Love Ka Jugaad

Vinod Naraen

FanatiXx
Publication

FanatiXx® Publication

Mumbai | Ahmedabad | Delhi NCR | Rourkela
ISO 9001:2015 Certified

By: Vinod Naraen

ISBN: 978-93-7406-955-4

Book: Love ka Jugaad
Price: INR 299/-

Printing By: BooksClub.in

Dedication

To my parents, Om and Shail, my first gurus who taught me the real definition of freedom and faith-

and to all those who donned on the robes of well-wishers to guide me when I needed it the most.

Foreword

What can one look for in a book that seems like a total giveaway in the very title of the novel, *Love ka Jugaad?* What can two star-crossed friends contribute towards yet another fiction read? Many such questions dotted my judging mind like most people, who wish to slot a rom-com into a folder which meant that the tale could be only one thing, love and nothing more. Fortunately for me, as well as for the innumerable people who shall be reading this book, I was happily proved wrong as I perused through the pages discovering that *Love Ka Jugaad* offered much more than I had expected.

Viraaj and Aneri are the two main characters of a romantic tale that flows with the witty, careless-carefree and sometimes hopelessly righteous optimism of the protagonist, Viraaj. He is not a person seeking love nor is he the one hastening the entire process of falling in love and pursuing the path of romance. He is the one who *rises* in love, simultaneously making others travelling with him (in soul and spirit) rise to the heights of joyful living. He shares his love. He shares joy.

Love Ka Jugaad moves like a journey besotted with the lack of expectations but pregnant with the joy of wishful experience and the satiation of sweet little desires. While it respects the laws of society it also rises up to express itself unabashedly when the occasion so demands. The protagonist could be any one of us – a teenager, a young adult, even a person older by age or vocation but unblemished by disappointment or cynicism of the world.

> ***"And, you know the saddest part? These people deserve our sympathy. Truly. Because imagine never learning empathy. Never learning brotherhood. Never learning to see beyond your own shelf of prizes. If you can't understand yourself, what good will you do for others?"***

Different tales of several people within this light hearted piece of fiction weave into each other like varied colored threads woven into one garment with a message that only pleads love, harmony, peace and the right to stay unprejudiced and fair.

What could have reeled off like a stereotypical story of romance of instant gratification transforms instead into a case of ideal representation of the current generation's view of life, of love, of roots, and of the right to debate for what is true.

Love Ka Jugaad is a tale that feels entirely relatable, wanting to be lived, loved, and reflected upon, permitting the protagonist to fight our case for us.

> ***We sat there a while longer, her guitar humming softly, my tumbler warming my hands, the mist curling around us like a secret. "You know," I said softly, "if you keep playing like this, I'll start believing life is actually a film."***

Shail Raghuvanshi

Poet and Author

Love Ka Jugaad is like a magical train journey where destiny leads two hearts to see the beauty in and beyond the ordinary and discover a new relationship within themselves...

Om Prakash Narayan,

An Indian Railway PR professional

A charming blend of humor, chaos, and romance, Love ka Jugaad captures the essence of Indian families and weddings with warmth.

Viraaj's quirks and Aneri's fire create a love story that is as hilarious as it is heartfelt.

The writing sparkles with cultural detail and witty banter.

A joyful, feel-good read that lingers long after the last page.

Devjyoti Barooah
Sr. Creative Director,

Gauge Advertising Ltd

INDEX

Vinod Naraen

Preface

Mornings in Chennai are never quiet. Temple bells clang against the honks of autos, vegetable vendors scream like news anchors, and a crow outside my window seems to think it is auditioning for Indian Idol.

I, Viraaj Naraen pronounced Naaraayan, twenty-four, future world-changing journalist and part-time chaos magnet, am stuffing socks into my suitcase while my family gives me a running commentary.

From the living room, Mumma calls out: "Viraaj! Did you pack your towel? Or you'll end up borrowing from cousins again!"

My mother, Shaily Raghuvanshi, wasn't scolding in anger—this was her love language. She was stirring *kheer* on the gas stove, humming an old Kishore Kumar tune in perfect rhythm. Usually, she hummed Hindi ghazals, sometimes Tamil classics, but this morning it was *Mere Sapno Ki Rani*.

From the balcony, Pa's voice cut through. "Viraaj! Don't make your train story into a comedy scene, remember, people struggle to laugh even a bit even if the jokes are funny! Just be yourself, that's more than *Madi*!

(Madi in Malayalam means 'enough', and since the family had lived in Palakkad in Kerala for the first eight years of Viraaj's life, everyone spoke bits and pieces of Malayalam here and there from time to time).

Prakash Narayan, my father, wasn't a man of uniform. As Senior Public Relations Officer in Southern Railways, he had too much influence to ever need one. Today he was in his usual style—crisp shirt tucked into jeans; sports shoes that looked brand new even though he'd had them for five years. He believed dressing simple. He believed it gave one credibility.

Meanwhile, in the corner of the hall, Naanu—my 92-year-old grandfather and self-proclaimed Sachin Tendulkar of memory—was bent over the sports page. His glasses slid down his nose as he muttered, "Rubbish fielding! Nobody in this generation knows how to spin a bowl!"

"Good morning, Naanu," I said, touching his feet.

He adjusted his glasses, grinning. "Morning, Betu. Win a kabaddi match or two in Shillong, okay? Don't just sit around cracking jokes or eating paneer."

I laughed. Only Naanu could reduce a cousin's wedding into a kabaddi trial.

Mumma appeared with a small steel bowl of dahi-cheeni—curd mixed with sugar. She held it up like it was prasaad.

"For shubh shuruaat," (auspicious beginnings) she said, feeding me a spoonful. "Sweet journey means sweet memories."

"Mumma, I'm twenty-four, not twelve," I protested.

She gave me *the* look. "Even at sixty-four, you'll still eat *dahi-cheeni* if I give it to you. Now shut up and finish it."

I obeyed. Honestly, who says no to curd and sugar anyway?

Just then, my phone buzzed. Caller ID: Palani Anna.

"Dei, Superstar!" his familiar gravelly voice boomed the moment I picked up. "Ready aa? Or still looking for your toothbrush under the sofa?"

"Ready, Anna," I said, laughing. "Come fast, or Pa will start writing a press release saying I missed the train."

Minutes later, the horn of his auto echoed through the street. I hugged Mumma, shook hands with Pa, then he pulled me into a bear- hug, and I let Naanu adjust my collar like I was entering an exam hall.

"Play straight," Naanu muttered, cricket still on his mind. "And don't let silly relatives bowl you out with marriage questions."

"Yes, Naanu," I said.

Downstairs, Palani Anna's auto waited. He was sixty-eight, forever in his jeans, auto driver khaki shirt, looking like a retired Rajinikanth in disguise. He'd been driving me since my 12th grade—college, dates, protests, even heartbreaks. More than an auto driver, he was family.

"Climb in, thambi," he said, tapping the seat like a drum.

As we rattled toward Chennai Central, he launched into his trademark lecture. "Don't create any trouble at the wedding, okay? Don't go giving speeches, fighting with waiters, or chasing girls like film heroes. Just eat well, dance two steps, and come back alive."

I grinned. "Anna, when have I *ever* created trouble?"

He nearly swerved into a cyclist. "Since 2016. Every year without fail."

We both burst out laughing.

Then I added softly, "Anna, you're still taking your BP medicines on time, right?"

He pretended to be annoyed. "Ayyo! Now you're acting like my doctor. Yes, yes, I shall take them regularly. Don't worry."

Soon, the grand arches of Chennai Central Railway Station came into view—red bricks glowing in the sun, platforms buzzing, kids crying, porters balancing luggage like circus performers.

I paid Anna, who gave me a mock salute. "Go, Superstar! Who knows—you might find your heroine on this train!"

"Anna, it's just a wedding," I said, shaking my head.

He winked. "In India, weddings *are* where heroines appear."

And with that, his auto sputtered away into the crowd.

What I didn't know then was that this wasn't just a train journey to Shillong.
It was a one-way ticket to chaos, comedy, music, and maybe... love.

Milk at the Railway Station

Yes, you got me.

My name is Viraaj.

Don't confuse me with the fancy actor whose name ends with Kapoor, like Viraj Kapoor. He has muscles, cars, and Bollywood. I have a pot belly from milk, a scooter I can't ride, and an electronics repair kit I never bought but somehow own.

I am Chennai-based and right now, standing at Chennai Central Railway Station with a suitcase in one hand and a bottle of milk in the other.

Yes, milk. Don't judge. I don't drink tea or coffee. I have tried both. Bitter. Life is bitter enough, why drink it too?

The loudspeaker announced: *"Train number 12509, Guwahati Express, platform number seven..."*

That's my train. Destination: Shillong.

Mission: Cousin's wedding.

Reward: Surviving five days with relatives who ask the same three questions—

1. "Beta, when are you getting married?"
2. "Beta, how much is your salary?"
3. "Beta, why do you still drink milk like a five-year-old?"

I dragged my suitcase across the platform, half-distracted by the chaos—hawkers yelling "chai-chai," porters balancing luggage on their heads, and an uncle arguing about reservations.

And then... I saw her.

She stood near the train door, one blue earphone dangling from her ear; she chewing gum like it was an Olympic sport. Her hair danced a little in the humid Chennai breeze. She was tall, confident, and had the kind of face that makes you think she can either save the world or destroy it—depending on her mood.

I froze. My legs said, *"Walk."* My brain said, *"Don't embarrass me."* My heart said, *"Say something filmy."*

Before I could decide, she caught me staring.

"Are you lost?" she asked, sharp.

"No," I said quickly. "I'm... directionally challenged."

She tilted her head. "So, basically lost."

Her sarcasm hit me harder than a cricket ball to the face. But I tried to recover. “Actually, I’m in the S3 coach. Just making sure this train is... um... safe.”

She smirked. “Wow. And here I was, thinking Indian Railways appointed guards. Turns out it’s you—Milkman of Chennai.”

My eyes widened. “How do you know about the milk part?”

She pointed at the bottle in my hand.

Right. I forgot I was holding it.

I mumbled, “It’s... protein.”

She laughed. A proper laugh. Loud enough that a passing uncle turned to look at us disapprovingly.

That laugh... I didn’t know it then, but it was going to follow me for a very long time.

The train whistled. People started pushing into the train. My suitcase got stuck between two aunties. Someone stepped on my shoe. My milk bottle almost fell.

And through all that, she stood there, calm, watching me struggle like I was free entertainment.

Finally, I squeezed in beside her.

“First time to Shillong?” I asked, trying to sound casual.

She raised an eyebrow. “Why? Do I look like I need a tour guide?”

“No, no,” I said quickly. “Just... conversation. For the journey.”

She looked at me for a second. Then, extended her hand.

"Aneri," she said.

"Viraaj," I replied, shaking her hand in return. My palm was sweaty. Not because of the Chennai heat. Because Aneri's smile had just short-circuited something in me.

And that's how my train ride—and maybe my life—changed forever.

Train Troubles

The Guwahati Express lurched forward like a reluctant buffalo, and humanity rearranged itself in layers: luggage, elbows, emotions, then me, wedged in the middle.

Aunty #1: "Beta, keep my steel dabba."
Aunty #2: "*Beta, aur upar chadhaa do.*" (Son, keep it more up)
Me: "Main... gravity ka dost hoon (I am a friend of gravity) aunty. Not anti-gravity."

Aneri, already near our row, watched with that anthropologist expression she had. Curiosity with a tinge of sarcasm.

I finally flopped on to my berth, a lower one.

Across: a snoring uncle warming up like a generator.

Above him: a child dangling headfirst to test mortality.

Aneri slid into the seat opposite. "So, Milkman of Chennai, what's the mission in Shillong?"

"Cousin's wedding," I said. "You?"

She shrugged. "Wedding."

"Whose?"

"Cousin."

We stared. Then laughed the awkward laugh of two people unknowingly approaching a twist.

The coach lights flickered twice and died. The tiny fans above sighed to a stop. Heat rose like a personal vendetta.

Groans erupted.

"Yaar, abhi se bijli gayi?" (Hey man, electricity has gone out already?)

"Arrey, TT ko bulao!" (Call the TT)

Somewhere, a baby began negotiations with the universe.

I stood up before my brain could stop me. "One minute," I said, more to myself than anyone. I climbed onto the seat edge, unscrewed the plastic cover near the fan switch with a coin, peered into a tangle of wires like a mystic reading tea leaves he doesn't drink.

Aneri folded her arms. "Please tell me you're not about to electrocute yourself."

"I'm tech-savvy," I said.

"You're tech-*lucky*," she corrected. "There's a difference."

I pinched a loose connector, tapped the relay with my knuckle (ancient rite), tore a strip of foil from a biscuit wrapper someone offered like prasaad, and snugged it into place.

The lights flared back to life. Fans whooshed. The coach cheered.

Snoring Uncle blinked awake and saluted me by mistake.

A kid whispered, awe-struck, "Iron Man!"

I sat, sheepish. Aneri leaned in. "How did you...?"

I shrugged. "Electrons and I are in a long-term relationship."

She smirked. "Are you this lucky with people?"

"Working on that."

The TT arrived; moustache loaded with authority. "Who touched the panel?"

I raised a hand like a student confessing to undone homework. He stared. Then, nodded. "Achha kaam. (Good work). Don't do that again." He scribbled something; a half smile hidden under the rulebook.

As the train settled into its metal lullaby, the great ritual of seat confusion began. Two families claimed the middle berth. An elderly gentleman insisted his ticket said "window bed," which is not a thing.

"Viraaj," Aneri said softly, tilting her chin toward two teenage girls juggling bags along the aisle. Their berth had been commandeered by an uncle expanding like an empire.

I stood. "Uncle ji, yeh unka seat..." (this is their seat) I started politely.

He waved me away. "Main kal se yahan hoon." (I am here from yesterday)

"Par aaj unka hai." (But, today, it is theirs) I smiled. "Kal ke liye main seat garam rakh dunga." (I shall warm the seat for tomorrow).

He glowered. Aneri stepped beside me, calm. "Uncle, agar aap yahan rahenge na, toh hum dono gaane gaayenge. (If you are here then we both will sing songs) *Loudly.*"

I nodded gravely. "I do Carnatic."

She added, "I do rock."

The uncle stared, measured the combined threat of shruti and shriek, then, surrendered with dignity. "Theek hai, theek hai."(Okay. Okay)

The girls mouthed thanks. Aneri didn't look at me, but I could feel her smile like a warm filament.

Later, boxes opened, paraathaas emerged, smells mingled. A kindly aunty offered me tea. I panicked. "Milk, please."

She blinked. "You want... doodh (milk)?"

"Yes." I braced for judgement.

She beamed. "Wah, sanskaari ladka! Arrey, Sushila, doodh laao!" (What a cultured boy! Oh Sushila get some milk!)

Within minutes, I had a steel tumbler big enough to bathe a cat. Aneri watched, amused. “You know, most guys act cool with black coffee.”

“I’ll act cool with calcium,” I said, sipping foam like it was champagne. “Cheers.”

She clinked her water bottle. “To our mutual... weddings?”

“Wait,” I said, pausing mid-sip. “Mutual?”

She narrowed her eyes. “Which side is your cousin?”

“Mom’s side,” I said. “Banarasi branch. The bride’s family is in Shillong.”

She squinted like she was focusing a camera. “Bride’s name?”

I took out my phone. Dead. Because destiny likes comedy.

I pulled out a power bank from my bag. Dead too. Less destiny, more stupidity.

“May I?” she said, holding out her phone. “Name?”

I told her. She typed. Notifications flooded like the monsoon. Her face changed from casual to... oh.

She turned the screen to me. A WhatsApp group: “Mukhim–Raghuvanshi Wedding: Mehendi Schedule”. A photo of a grinning couple.

The bride was my cousin. The groom’s surname... Mukhim.

(For context: The majority of communities in Meghalaya, including the Khasi, Jaintia, and Garo, are matrilineal, meaning lineage is traced through the mother. Traditionally, children adopt their mother's clan name, a practice that is a significant aspect of identity.)

We stared at the pixels.

"So," she said slowly, "my cousin is marrying your cousin."

I set the milk down before it set me down. "Plot twist."

"One coach, two cousins, one wedding," she said. "Try explaining that to astrology."

"Or Indian Railways," I said.

We laughed. The universe, satisfied, shook the train gently.

Somewhere past midnight, a minor calamity struck. The uncle who had earlier surrendered a seat was now battling a phone possessed by demons; its speaker blasted "Baby Doll" at full volume and would not stop. Buttons failed. The screen froze. Panic spread.

"BETA!" he pleaded to the air in general. "Bund karo yey!" (Switch this off!)

I took the phone, thumbed the side, popped the SIM tray with a staple from my notebook, pressed power + volume combo, nothing. I pried the back half a millimetre, nudged the battery contact with the corner of my coin, and murmured, "Shanti."

Silence. The coach exhaled. The uncle patted my cheek like I was a successful harvest.

Aneri, eyes bright: "Okay, that was witchcraft. Right?"

"Just electrons," I said.

"Or they're in love with you," she said. "Machines, I mean."

"People?" I asked before my self-esteem filter could intervene.

She pretended to think, lips curling. "Jury's out."

We drifted into conversations that no one plans but everyone remembers—the stories you tell strangers because they won't judge, and the stories that make strangers less strange. She told me about Shillong rains that arrive like secrets, of guitar nights at cafés where the lights are fairy and the faces are free. I told her about Marina mornings, about temple bells sharing space with motorcycle horns, about a mother who can weaponize a WhatsApp forward.

"Do you always fix things?" she asked at some point, voice soft in the night's hammock.

"I try," I said. "Mostly by accident."

"And people?"

"I break them less than I used to." I smiled. "Work in progress."

She nodded. "Same."

We didn't sleep so much as blink in long intervals. The train kept time, the tracks sang their metal lullaby, and far ahead, Shillong waited with hills, relatives, and a wedding that would be too big to be only one thing.

At dawn, when light unwrapped the coach, Aneri leaned down from her berth and poked my shoulder.

"Hey, Milkman."

"Yes?"

"Don't tell anyone yet," she said, mischief alive. "Let's reveal the cousin-connection at the house. It'll be fun."

"Drama," I said, hand to heart. "My mother would approve."

"Good," she said, then, added, "Also... thanks for the fans, the phone, and the seat revolution."

I grinned. "Anytime. I do subscriptions."

She rolled her eyes. "Jury's narrowing."

The train curved, the sun poured gold on sleeping faces, and for a moment, I felt—ridiculous as it sounds—plugged in. To the coach. To the rails. To a girl who folded sarcasm into kindness like a practiced origami.

Ahead of us were the hills.

Between us was a secret.

Around us was India—loud, generous, impossible, and home.

A Shared Seat - A Shared Story

By morning, the Guwahati Express had settled into its rhythm: chai-sellers announcing themselves like politicians, babies revealing their presence like rock bands, and people brushing their teeth on the platform at every other stop.

My berth was now occupied by three aunties, two children, and one mountain of luggage. My bag had migrated to a place under a stranger's feet. My milk bottle had rolled over under someone's berth like a lost pet.

Basically, my seat was gone.

"Excuse me," I said to the universe.
The universe ignored me.

Aneri peeked down from her upper berth, smirking. "Lost your kingdom, Your Majesty?"

"Democracy failed me," I said gravely. "Any spare territory up there?"

She sighed, scooted over, and patted the space beside her. "Come on. But if you snore, I'll throw you out."

I climbed up awkwardly, nearly kicking a sleeping uncle. Aneri shook her head. "Graceful. Very graceful."

I settled in, trying to look casual. She pulled her legs up, hugging them, chin resting on her knees. I mirrored her; except I immediately got a cramp. Smooth.

"So, Viraaj," she said. "What's your deal? Chennai or Banaras?"

"Both," I said. "Father from Chennai. Mother from Banaras. I'm like... sambhar poured over kachori."

She burst out laughing. "That's horrible—and brilliant."

"Story of my life," I said. "At school, I was the guy who could sing Carnatic ragas *and* recite shaayari. Nobody knew what to do with me. Except in kabaddi—I just confused the opponents until they tripped."

"And now?" she asked, tilting her head.

"Now I fix fans and phones accidentally. I'm basically a walking service centre. Except, I can't drive. Cars, bikes, scooters—nope. Tried. Failed. Gravity loves me too much."

She chuckled. "So you're a... poet-engineer-singer-who-can't-drive."

"Correct," I said. "And you?"

Her smile softened. “Shillong girl. Music runs in the family. My cousins all play something—guitar, drums, whatever makes noise. I sing sometimes, but mostly... I like to listen. And write.”

“Write what?” I asked, curious.

“Little things. Observations. Lines that make me laugh, or hurt, or feel less invisible.”

“Invisible?” I frowned.

She shrugged. “When people know you’re from the North East, they either don’t know what to say, or they say the wrong thing. Like, ‘Do you eat dog?’ Or, ‘China se ho kya?’ (Are you from China?) It gets onto your nerves.”

Her voice was steady, but her eyes were sharp, like she had rehearsed this explanation too many times.

“I’m sorry,” I said quietly.

“Don’t be,” she said. “Just... listen. That’s enough.”

And so, I listened.

For the first time, the sarcasm between us thinned, and I saw her—not as the girl with the gum and the smirk, but as someone who carried her world with equal pride and weariness.

We might have sat in that pocket of silence longer, but destiny—also known as Coach S3—had other plans.

A commotion started at the far end of the coach. Two men in leather jackets were arguing with the ticket collector. Their voices rose, their gestures sharper. Passengers shrank back. One man shoved the TT, who stumbled.

The uncle next to me muttered, "Goondas. (Thugs)"

Aneri's hand froze on her knee. I felt the coach tighten like a drum.

Before my brain could apply brakes, my body stood up. "Arrey, stop it! This is a train, not WWE!"

Everyone turned. Including the goondas.

Fantastic!

The taller one sneered. "And who are you?"

"Just another passenger in the train" I declared, my voice trembling but my hand somehow holding my half-empty milk bottle like a weapon.

They blinked. Confusion bought me three seconds.

In those three seconds, the train jerked around a curve. I lost balance, stumbled forward—

—and my elbow jabbed straight into the tall guy's stomach.

He wheezed, doubled over. His partner tried to grab me, but in the chaos my foot hooked under a water canister. It rolled across the floor, tripping him.

Both men crashed down. Luggage fell on them for dramatic effect.

The coach erupted in applause. Kids cheered. The TT dusted himself off and declared, "Hero!"

I stood there, stunned. Aneri's eyes were wide, then, narrowed with amusement.

"You..." she said slowly, "are the clumsiest hero I've ever seen."

I grinned sheepishly. "Told you. Accidental service centre. Even for justice."

She shook her head, laughing, and for the first time, it felt like maybe—just maybe—the jury on me was leaning toward approval.

The coach was still buzzing from my accidental stunt. People were whispering "Hero" like it was my surname. The goondas had been handed off at the next station, the TT gave me a pat on the back, and the aunties offered me aaloo (potato) paraathaas like victory medals.

I sat back down, heart still sprinting. Aneri, across from me, crossed her arms.

"So," she said, deadpan, "you're a fighter now?"

"Not really," I said. "More like... gravity's favourite weapon."

She chuckled, shaking her head. "I don't get you. One second you're fixing fans with biscuit foil, next second you're defeating rowdies with... what, milk power?"

"Calcium-fortified elbows," I said, raising mine. "Very much underrated."

She laughed again, then, tilted her head, curious. "Okay, seriously. Who are you, Viraaj?"

I hesitated, then, decided honesty couldn't hurt. "I'm a journalist."

Her eyes widened a little. "Journalist? Really?"

"Yeah. Chennai Chronicle," I said, straightening. "Don't get too impressed—it's mostly city beat. Protests, potholes, politicians cutting ribbons."

"But that explains..." she said, trailing off.

"Explains what?"

"Why you notice things," she replied. "Why you talk like you're narrating a story."

I blinked. No one had ever said that to me before.

I smiled sheepishly. "Well, I guess I do collect stories. People, places, even broken gadgets. Everything has a story if you look."

"And what would mine be?" she asked, eyebrow arched.

I studied her for a moment. "Hmm. Girl from the hills. Laughs like thunder. Eyes like... those Shillong rains you talked about. But with edges—like you're always ready to prove something."

For a second, Aneri didn't reply. Her gum stilled. Her eyes softened.

"You're not bad," she said finally. "At noticing."

"Comes with the job," I said. "Journalists are professional eavesdroppers."

"Professional troublemakers too," she added.

"True," I admitted. "We write truths no one wants to read. Or sometimes, truths no one wants to admit about themselves."

The train rattled along. Outside, the world turned dark fields and nameless towns. Inside, people dozed, murmured, shifted. It felt like the world had shrunk to just the two of us and a faint smell of biryani.

"Tell me something," I said quietly. "Do you like Shillong?"

She leaned back. "I love it. But... sometimes I feel caged too. Everyone knows everyone. You can't hide. You can't reinvent. You just are what your family is."

I nodded slowly. "I get that. For me, it's the opposite. I'm split. Banaras mom, Chennai dad. Too South for the North, too North for the South. I fit everywhere and nowhere at the same time."

She turned to me, really turned, and studied me with those rainstorm eyes. "That's rough."

I shrugged. “Not always. Sometimes it’s fun. One day I’m eating curd rice, the next day kachori. But yeah... when you don’t belong fully, you’re always searching for... home, I guess.”

Silence stretched, but it wasn’t uncomfortable. Just heavy with something unnamed.

Then Aneri smiled crookedly. “You know, for someone who drinks milk out of steel tumblers, you’re pretty deep.”

I grinned. “Journalist, remember? We deal in depths. And, headlines.”

“Oh, yeah? Then what’s my headline?” she challenged.

I thought for a second, then said:

“‘Local Girl Outsmarts Milk-Drinking Hero on Train. Nation Laughs. Hero Cries.’”

She burst out laughing, clutching her stomach. “That’s terrible!”

“Accurate,” I said. “And tomorrow’s viral.”

She shook her head, still giggling. “God, you’re ridiculous.”

And somewhere between her laughter and the train’s rumble, I realized something dangerous: I liked being ridiculous. Especially if it made her laugh.

The coach had finally quieted. A few snores formed a chorus, punctuated by the occasional cough and the lullaby rhythm of wheels against tracks. Dim yellow lights flickered.

Aneri stretched out on her berth, leaning against her bag. I sat cross-legged across from her, holding my empty milk bottle like it was a relic from war.

“Alright, Milkman,” she said, voice lower, softer. “Since sleep is clearly avoiding us, let’s play a game.”

I perked up.

She rolled her eyes. “Truth or Dare.”

I blinked. “You... want to play truth or dare on a train?”

“Why not?” she shrugged. “Best time. Strangers around us, moving metal box, nowhere to escape.”

“Comforting,” I muttered. “Fine. But no dares involving running outside.”

“Relax,” she said with a mischievous grin. “Truth first. Why do you only drink milk?”

“Easy,” I said. “Chai is bitter, coffee is bitter. Milk is simple. Honest. Like me.”

She smirked. “Simple? Honest? Says the guy who elbowed a goon into submission by accident.”

“Hey, accidents count as honesty,” I argued. “Okay, my turn. Truth: What’s one thing people get totally wrong about you?”

She was thoughtful. “That I’m always strong. People think sarcasm equals invincibility. But actually...” She paused, biting her lip. “Sometimes I just use it so no one sees I’m scared.”

I didn't say anything. Just nodded. Sometimes silence speaks better.

She cleared her throat. "Okay, Dare."

I looked around. "Here? Now?"

"Yes. Dare: Sing me something. Carnatic or shaayari. Dealer's choice."

I groaned. "You're evil."

She smirked. "Thank you."

I thought for a second, and then cleared my throat. "Okay, but don't blame me if people complain."

I sang—not perfectly, but earnestly. A short Carnatic phrase my father had drilled into me since childhood. My voice wasn't concert material, but in the half-dark, it felt... okay. True.

Aneri listened, head tilted, eyes softer than I'd seen them all day. When I stopped, embarrassed, she clapped lightly.

"Not bad, Milkman," she said. "Not bad at all."

I smiled sheepishly. "Thanks. Okay, your turn. Truth: What's the silliest thing you've ever done at a wedding?"

She grinned instantly. "Easy. At my cousin's wedding last year, I switched the groom's sherwaani (a knee-length coat closed up to the neck, worn by men in India) pocket square with one made out of toilet paper. He didn't notice until the photo session."

I burst out laughing, clutching my stomach. "That's... evil genius level."

"Family tradition," she said with mock pride.

We kept going, trading little secrets like cards.

I admitted I once accidentally published a typo in a newspaper headline that said *"Mayor opens new pubic park."*

She nearly choked laughing. "PUBIC?"

"Don't remind me," I groaned. "My editor nearly killed me. The memes still haunt me."

She confessed she once ate five plates of momos in a contest and then sang karaoke until she threw up onstage.

By the time we'd run out of dares, something had shifted. We weren't just passengers anymore. We were co-conspirators against the night.

Finally, she asked, softly, "Truth: What do you really want, Viraaj? Like... in life."

The train clattered, giving me time. I looked down at my hands.

"I want," I said slowly, "to find a place where I don't feel like half-and-half. A place where... I belong. Where someone looks at me and says, 'You're enough.'"

It was too raw. Too honest. I wanted to take it back.

But Aneri didn't laugh. She didn't tease. She just held my gaze. "Maybe you don't need a place," she said quietly. "Maybe you just need a person."

The words hung between us, heavier than any luggage in the coach.

And for the first time in a very long time, I wondered if maybe, just maybe, the person was sitting right across from me.

Arrival in Shillong

The train groaned into Guwahati just as dawn cracked open the sky, spilling pale pink light over everything. “Wake up, Milkman,” Aneri nudged me with that smirk playing on her lips. “We’re here.”

Groggy, I blinked at the platform outside—hawkers balancing flasks, coolies sprinting, families waving from behind railings.

“This is... Guwahati?” I mumbled.

“Congratulations,” she deadpanned. “Geography: passed.”

Dragging our suitcases, we pushed through the sea of elbows and luggage. The air felt different already—cooler, scented faintly of tea leaves and rain. Even the sunlight had a softer edge.

We made our way past the taxi queue and found a shared cab headed toward Shillong. The driver, chewing betel asked, “Doh (two) passengers?”

“Yes,” Aneri said. Then, glancing at me, added with mock irritation, “And one milk bottle.”

I muttered under my breath, "National-level bullying."

The cab joined the long line of vehicles snaking out of the station. Soon, Guwahati's din faded, replaced by roads climbing into hills that stretched like folded green silk.

The taxi to Shillong—four hours of winding roads, pine forests, and fog so thick it looked like the world was hiding secrets.

I sat in the backseat, pressed between two uncles and a suitcase that smelled like pickles. Aneri was up front, hair tied in a messy bun, humming something under her breath that made the whole journey feel like a music video.

I pressed my forehead to the glass. Villages passed by—tiny tea stalls, schoolchildren in uniforms chasing each other, mist slipping between the pines like a shy guest.

Mumma's voice came back to me in memory: *Beta, travel with open eyes. Every new place is a story waiting to be told.*

I smiled faintly. "Pa always said trains were like classrooms."

"But these hills..." I exhaled. "They feel like poetry."

Aneri turned her head, watching me with that expression halfway between mockery and something softer. "Careful, Milkman. Too much poetry, and you'll drown in the mist."

I grinned. "Better than drowning in bitter coffee."

She laughed—sharp, unguarded, genuine. The kind that made strangers in the cab glance back, curious.

As the road twisted higher, she gestured toward a bend where the clouds seemed to hang low enough to touch. “This,” she said, her voice quieter now, “is what I grew up with. Shillong isn’t just hills and guitars. It’s... home.”

I turned to her. “Then thanks for bringing me home, even if by accident.”

Her lips twitched. “Drama king.”

But she looked out the window again, hiding a smile.

And just like that, Shillong welcomed us—not with grand announcements, but with misty roads, pine forests, and the promise of stories waiting to unfold.

By the time we reached Shillong, the city was waking—tea stalls steaming, school kids in sweaters running along narrow lanes, and a sudden drizzle that came out of nowhere like an uninvited guest.

The taxi pulled into a big house alive with colour. Strings of marigolds hung from the gate, the courtyard buzzed with relatives, and loudspeakers tested microphones with the usual *“Hello? One, two, three...”* echo.

I stepped out, suitcase in one hand, milk bottle in the other. My mother’s cousin, the bride’s father, spotted me immediately.

“Arrey, Viraaj! Beta, you came!” He pulled me into a bear hug before shouting over his shoulder. “Varuna! See, your nephew has arrived!”

And just like that, I was swallowed into the madness. Aunties pulling my cheeks and saying, "Kitna bada ho gaya!" (You have become so big), cousins demanding gifts, and kids asking if I'd brought chocolates.

I barely managed to breathe when I heard it—Aneri's voice, somewhere behind me.

"Ma, I'm here!" she called, dragging her bag across the gate.

I turned. She froze. We stared at each other like two actors who'd just realized they were in the wrong movie.

Then her cousin, the groom, came bounding down the steps. "Aneri! Finally!" He hugged her, then, spotted me. "Arrey Viraaj bhaiya! You made it too!"

He slung an arm around each of us. "Perfect. Two sides of the family, united. Welcome to the wedding house!"

I blinked. Aneri blinked. At the same time, we blurted:

"YOU'RE the bride's cousin?"
"YOU'RE the groom's cousin?"

The groom laughed, clueless. "Yes, yes! What a coincidence, na? It is a small world!"

"Small world," Aneri muttered under her breath, shooting me a look that was half amusement, half murder.

The courtyard erupted in fresh chaos as more relatives piled on. Someone shoved sweets into my hand, another tried to balance a garland around my neck, and an aunty yelled, "Beta, put your suitcase in the upstairs room, fast!"

I staggered through the crowd, trying to process the cosmic joke. Not only had Aneri and I met on the train, not only had we bonded over truth-or-dare confessions, but now... we were officially family.

Distant, complicated, extended family—but family.

Inside, the house was a circus. Women sat cross-legged on the floor, sorting flowers into baskets. Men argued over decorations. Kids ran in circles like sugar-fuelled rockets.

In the middle of it all, I saw Aneri, surrounded by her side of the family. She looked different here—softer, lighter, laughing as her aunts teased her about "helping with the groom's side."

One of her little cousins tugged her sleeve and pointed at me. "Didi (Sister), who's that boy?"

Aneri followed his finger. Our eyes met across the room.

For a second, time slowed.

She rolled her eyes at me. I raised my milk bottle in salute.

She tried not to laugh. Failed.

And just like that, the Shillong wedding chaos had its newest subplot: Viraaj and Aneri, co-cousins, accidental allies, and maybe something neither of us was ready to admit yet.

The minute my suitcase hit the floor of the courtyard, I was captured.

Not politely welcomed but c*aptured.*

One aunty seized my arm. "Arrey, Viraaj beta! Kitna bada ho gaya! Last time I saw you, you were in chaddi (shorts)."

Another aunty appeared from nowhere, pinching my cheek like I was still five. "Such a handsome boy! Drinking milk worked, na?"

Before I could respond, a wiry uncle with oil-slicked hair asked, "Beta, journalist ho na? Achha batao, (Okay, tell me) this new government… is it good or bad?"

I stammered, "Uh, I—"

"Bad, of course bad," another uncle interrupted, wagging his finger. "Write against them, beta! Your pen is your sword!"

"I usually write about potholes," I muttered, but nobody heard me.

Just then, an older cousin swooped in, eyeing my suitcase. "Viraaj bhaiya (brother), please tell me you brought duty-free alcohol from the airport?"

"I came by train."

He looked at me like I'd confessed to murder. "Train?!" He slapped his forehead and walked away in disgust.

Meanwhile, a gaggle of aunties surrounded me, firing questions like rapid gunshots:

"Salary kitna hai?" (How much is your salary?)
"Office mein koi ladki pasand aayi kya?" (Did you like any girl in your office?)
"You still drink only milk? Not good for shaadi (married) life!"
"Beta, your hair is thinning. Take bhringraaj oil (false daisy oil)."

I opened my mouth, but words failed.

Across the courtyard, Aneri leaned against a pillar, watching me drown in relatives. Her grin stretched from Shillong to Chennai.

I mouthed, *Help me!*

She mouthed back, *No chance.* Then, added a mock salute, like she was wishing me luck in war.

Before I could escape, a group of kids surrounded me like tiny sharks.

"Bhaiya, play kabaddi with us!" one demanded.
"Tell us a ghost story!" another shouted.
"Fix my remote car, it's broken!" the youngest whined, shoving a toy into my hands.

I sighed, squatting down with the toy car. A loose wire, a dead battery, a quick shake—and it whirred back to life.

The kids gasped like I'd just invented electricity.

"WIZARD!" one of them screamed, running to announce it to the entire household.

More people crowded around me. An aunty handed me a faulty mixer-grinder. An uncle gave me his Nokia phone that hadn't switched on since 2008. Within ten minutes, I was sitting cross-legged in the middle of the courtyard like a roadside mechanic-slash-magician, fixing gadgets while everyone clapped.

Someone even shouted, "Viraaj beta, after the wedding, open shop here only!"

I looked up in desperation.

Aneri was watching, sipping chai elegantly. When she saw me glaring, she raised her cup like a toast.

"Oh, this is too good," she said, walking over. "The Milkman of Chennai, now the Electrician of Shillong."

"You could at least pretend to rescue me," I hissed under my breath.

"And miss this free entertainment? Never."

One of her aunts pulled her closer. "Aneri, you know this boy?"

She gave me a side glance, a wicked smile playing on her lips. "Yes, Maasi. He's... my train friend."

"Train friend?" the aunt echoed, delighted. "Wah, wah! Train mein hi dosti ho gayi! (You became friends on the train itself!) Who knows, kal kya hoga?" (What will happen tomorrow?)

The aunt winked. Aneri smirked. I nearly choked on my own tongue.

By the time evening arrived, I had fixed a total of 3 fans, 2 phones, 1 broken microphone and the self-respect of one small boy whose toy car now zoomed like a Ferrari.

Everyone was happy. Everyone except me—because Aneri hadn't stopped teasing once.

"Careful, Viraaj," she said sweetly as I carried my suitcase upstairs. "If you keep this up, they'll make you the wedding electrician, wedding singer, and wedding bodyguard all at once."

I sighed dramatically. "And you? What's your grand role?"

She smiled innocently. "Bride's cousin, groom's cousin… and apparently, your personal critic."

I groaned.

She laughed.

And that's how my official induction into Shillong wedding chaos began—with relatives grilling me alive, gadgets piling at my feet, and Aneri standing there, enjoying every second of my humiliation.

The wedding house was chaos. Loud, colourful, endlessly buzzing—like a festival, a cricket match, and a music concert rolled into one.

I had barely survived three aunties tugging me toward the dessert counter when I stumbled into the backyard, looking for oxygen.

And there they were.

Riya—the bride, my cousin—draped in a simple kurta for the pre-functions, hair tied up, mischief sparkling in her eyes. Next to her, Arvind—the groom, Aneri's cousin looking harassed but deeply in love. And Aneri, of course, leaning against a pillar like sarcasm was her oxygen.

"Viraaj bhaiya!" Riya squealed, rushing in to hug me. "Finally. My partner-in-crime has arrived."

"Correction," Arvind muttered. "Your partner-in-chaos."

I shook his hand. "Chaos is underrated. Builds character."

Aneri piped in sweetly, "And headlines. Don't forget, he is a journalist."

We gathered on the terrace with paper cups of juice. The four of us fell into an easy rhythm: Riya tossing jokes like grenades, Arvind catching them with deadpan comebacks, Aneri smirking at my expense, me retaliating with exaggerated dramatics.

"Tell us," Riya demanded, "are you going to crack wedding jokes on stage?"

"Only if you let me charge entry," I said.

"Entry?" Arvind frowned.

"Yeah," I grinned. "Family discounts available. But no refunds if offended."

Aneri laughed so suddenly that even she looked startled.

That moment—four of us laughing together—it felt like déjà vu of a movie scene I'd once watched. The kind where strangers become friends, weddings become adventures, and love sneaks in through banter.

The wedding quartet was born.

By the time the house quieted, I was half-dead.

Three aunties had fed me plates of pakoraas until my stomach filed a complaint, two uncles had cornered me into a political debate I barely survived, and five kids had begged me to fix their toy robot until I caved in.

Finally, silence. The courtyard emptied, fairy lights blinked lazily in the mist, and the air smelled of pine and leftover samosaas.

I stepped outside, needing air. My milk bottle was almost empty, but I held it like a comfort weapon.

That's when I saw her. Again.

Aneri was sitting on the stone steps at the edge of the courtyard, knees tucked to her chest, looking up at the night sky. The glow from the lights touched her hair, making her look like she belonged to both the house and the hills.

I walked over, sat a few steps below her. "So, did you enjoy the show?"

She looked down, lips curving into a grin. "Very much. You should have seen your face when Maasi (maternal aunt) asked about your thinning hair."

I groaned. “That was cruelty.”

“Honesty,” she corrected. “Family is like that. Cuts deeper than scissors.”

I took a sip of milk, then, held it up to her like a toast. “Well, here’s to surviving Day One.”

She shook her head. “You’re unbelievable. Everyone else is drinking chai, coffee, wine… you show up with a milk bottle like it’s champagne.”

“Milk is honest,” I said. “No caffeine, no drama. Just… comfort.”

She tilted her head, watching me. “You know, it actually suits you.”

“Milk?”

“No,” she said, smiling faintly. “Being… different. You don’t even try, and still…”

I raised an eyebrow. “Still what?”

She shrugged, looking away at the mist curling over the trees. “Still… people notice.”

For a second, I didn’t know what to say. So I went for my default-defence. Humour.

“Not always. Back in Chennai, I’m basically invisible. Journalists aren’t movie stars, you know. We just chase people who refuse to talk and then write about potholes.”

She glanced back at me. "Invisible? You? Viraaj, you couldn't be invisible even if you tried. You walk into a room and immediately trip over something. That's not invisibility—that's... chaos."

"Chaos?" I said, pretending to be offended.

"Funny chaos," she corrected softly.

We sat there, the quiet wrapping around us. Somewhere inside, a relative coughed. Somewhere outside, a stray dog barked. The hills hummed their night song.

I broke the silence. "Truth or Dare—just one last round off the record."

She smirked. "Fine. Truth."

I leaned closer. "Do you actually like me, or are you just having me around for comic benefit?"

Her eyes met mine, steady, glinting. Then she grinned. "Both."

I laughed, shaking my head. "Fair enough."

"And you?" she asked suddenly. "Truth. Why did you really get on this train? You could have skipped the wedding. Families forget."

I hesitated, then, sighed. "Because... I didn't want to be forgotten. Not this time. I wanted to belong somewhere, even if it's noisy and messy and people call me Milkman."

She didn't tease. She didn't laugh. She just looked at me for a long, quiet moment.

Then, softly, she said, "Maybe you already do."

Before I could reply, a voice boomed from the house: "Aneri! Viraaj! Come inside, children! Tomorrow is Mehendi (Henna)! Sleep now, gossip later!"

We both jumped, startled.

Aneri smirked. "Saved by the aunty."

I smiled, standing. "Story of my life."

We walked back inside, side by side, shoulders brushing just slightly—enough to make my heart do that strange little skip it had started learning to do ever since I met her.

The Wedding Circus (The Mehendi Avoiders)

If chaos had a ringtone, it would sound like an Indian wedding.

I woke up to drums, laughter, and the smell of snacks. When I stumbled into the courtyard, the whole house was a buzzing anthill. Aunties sat in circles, hands stretched, palms glistening with mehendi. Kids ran around with cones of henna like it was Holi. Loudspeakers tested mics with *"one-two, check, hello, hello."*

And then it hit me: today was the dreaded Mehendi Ceremony.

My nightmare.

Why? Because mehendi stains everything it touches—hands, clothes, dignity. And once it's on you, it refuses to leave, like clingy relatives.

I tried to quietly sneak toward the food counter (the safest corner of any wedding). But of course, an aunty spotted me.

"Viraaj beta! Come, sit! We'll put mehendi on your hands also!"

I panicked. "Aunty, I... I'm allergic!"

She gasped. "To mehendi?"

"Yes," I blurted. "Severe allergy. My... um... fingers swell like balloons."

She looked suspicious. "Really?"

"Yes! Last time someone tried, my hand looked like... like a pumpkin!"

Another aunty overheard. "Pumpkin? Arrey, don't exaggerate!"

The first aunty clucked her tongue. "Still, no risks. Fine, beta. You go eat."

Relieved, I scurried away—only to nearly bump into Aneri, who was escaping from the opposite side.

She caught sight of me, eyes wide, then, burst out laughing. "Let me guess—mehendi ambush?"

"Close call," I muttered. "Apparently, I'm allergic.'"

She grinned. "Nice. I told them mehendi makes me faint. Worked like a charm."

I blinked. "Wait... you hate mehendi too?"

"Despise it," she said firmly. "Sticky, smelly, impossible to eat food without smearing your face. Plus, I don't need someone writing a random guy's initials on my palm for luck."

I chuckled. "Finally! Someone understands."

We slipped into the food section like conspirators in exile. The table was a glorious battlefield of samosas, jalebis, pakoraas, and momos. I reached for the momos first, but one bite into the chutney and my tongue burst into flames.

I coughed violently, reaching for water. Aneri handed me a steel glass, laughing. "Careful, Milkman. That chutney doesn't like outsiders."

"My tongue is suing me for negligence," I wheezed.

She popped a momo into her mouth effortlessly, shrugging. "Weakling."

I narrowed my eyes. "You're enjoying this, aren't you?"

"Very much," she said, smirking.

Before I could argue, a relative's booming voice called out: "Viraaj beta! Since you're the journalist, come, come! Ask the groom questions for us!"

And just like that, I was shoved into a chair across from the groom—Aneri's cousin, my cousin's soon-to-be husband while a circle of relatives watched like it was a press conference.

"Beta, ask him about love!" one uncle demanded.

I cleared my throat, channelling my inner reporter. "So... why did you fall in love with my cousin?"

The groom stammered. "Because... she laughs at my jokes?"

The crowd erupted in "Awwws."

I leaned in dramatically. “And are you prepared for a lifetime of nagging?”

Everyone roared with laughter. My cousin (the bride) shouted from upstairs, “He’d better be!”

I grinned. Across the courtyard, Aneri leaned against a pillar, arms crossed, watching the circus. When our eyes met, she mouthed; *you’re loving this, aren’t you?*

I mouthed back, *Help me.*

She mouthed back, *Nope.*

Later, as the mehendi frenzy reached its peak, we both found ourselves hiding again—this time behind the flower-storage room.

“Co-conspirators,” I said, raising my milk bottle in toast. “Escaping mehendi, one excuse at a time.”

She clinked her chai cup against it. “Allergic Pumpkin Boy and Fainting Girl. We’d make a great superhero duo.”

I laughed. “Our superpower? Avoiding henna stains.”

“Exactly,” she said, smiling wide.

And as the drums thumped louder, laughter spilling from the courtyard, we sat there—two outsiders, bonded not by mehendi on our palms, but by the relief of escaping it together.

The Sangeeth

Aneri caught me sneaking out of the house, notebook in hand.

"Planning to interview the goats outside?" she teased.

"Planning to breathe," I shot back. "Too many aunties inside. They're like investigative journalists, but scarier."

She chuckled. "Come on then, Milkman. Time to see my Shillong."

We wandered through winding lanes, mist curling like lazy smoke. She pointed out tiny cafés where bands practiced, walls covered in rock posters, and stalls selling steaming momos.

At one stop, she bought two plates of momos, handing me one. "Eat. And don't say it needs chutney. This chutney can melt planets."

I took a bite, almost choked on the fire, and she laughed till she doubled over.

"Fine," I wheezed. "I accept defeat."

Later, we sat on a bench overlooking the hills. Clouds drifted like ships.

"So, Milkman," she said softly, "what do you really want?"

I thought. "To change the world word by word. Journalism, stand-up, writing... laughter can heal too, right? But, somewhere in there... I want love. Silly, ordinary, extraordinary love."

She looked at me, expression unreadable. "Not bad for a guy who can't ride a scooter."

"And you?" I asked.

Her voice softened. "Music. Writing songs that matter. Building something real in my career. And maybe... finding someone who won't be scared of my fire."

I smiled. "I'm lactose-tolerant to fire."

She burst out laughing, swatting my arm.

And under that misty Shillong sky, something shifted. Friendship deepened. Banter softened. Love hovered—unspoken, but very present.

The mehendi chaos gave way to bigger storms—the Sangeeth (Song) rehearsals.

If you've never witnessed Sangeeth prep, imagine an army drill where the weapons are dance moves and the battleground is ego. Bride's side versus groom's side. Songs, steps, glitter—winner takes glory.

Except this time, disaster struck.

The professional dance instructor hired to train the bride's side had vanished last minute—some emergency in Guwahati. Panic spread like wildfire. Aunties wrung their hands. The bride nearly cried.

"Arrey, ab kya hoga?" (what will happen now?) one cousin wailed. "The groom's side has Bollywood-level choreographers!"

That's when fifty pairs of eyes turned to me.

Me. Viraaj. Milkman. Tech mechanic. Non-driver.

"Viraaj beta," an aunty pleaded, clasping my hand. "You must help!"

"What?!" I squeaked. "I can't choreograph!"

Before I could protest any further, Aneri appeared at my side, grinning wickedly. "Yes, Milkman. Show us your hidden talents."

"I don't have hidden talents!" I said desperately.

"Then it's time to discover them," she smirked.

And so, with no escape, I became the official dance instructor of the bride's side.

What started as chaos turned into comedy. Uncles tripped over their own feet, aunties kept forgetting steps, and kids tried breakdancing in the middle of Bollywood routines.

But something lit up inside me. Maybe it was the challenge, maybe it was the journalist in me who liked organizing mess into stories, but within an hour, I had everyone in sync.

"Left, right, spin—smile! No aunty, don't smack him during the spin! Again, from the top!"

Aneri leaned against the doorframe, watching, her grin softening into something else.

And then came the grand finale: our main number. I picked a high-voltage track—"Current Laga Re" from *Cirkus (2022)***.** Loud, crazy, dramatic—the perfect anthem to shock the groom's side.

We rehearsed for hours. My sherwaani stuck to my back with sweat, but the more I taught, the more confident I became. By the end, everyone was cheering, high-fiving, and shouting, "Viraaj bhaiya, you're a genius!"

Even Aneri clapped slowly, mock-regal. "Well, well. Milkman has moves."

"Don't sound so surprised," I said, wiping sweat. "I've been secretly preparing for *Dance India Dance* auditions my whole life."

That night, under fairy lights and disco balls, the two sides clashed. The groom's side opened with a flashy medley—impressive, polished, and straight out of a music video. The crowd roared.

Then it was our turn.

We marched out like warriors. The opening beats of "Current Laga Re" dropped. And suddenly—BOOM. Energy, colour, chaos, rhythm. Aunties twirled like pros, uncles nailed the beats, and kids stole the spotlight with their jumps.

And me? I jumped in for the climax—front and centre, spinning, clapping, shouting "Current laga re!" with every ounce of drama in my body.

The crowd went wild. The groom's side paled. We'd won. No contest.

People lifted me onto their shoulders, chanting my name. "Viraaj! Viraaj!"

For the first time in my life, I felt like a Bollywood hero.

And in the corner, Aneri was laughing, clapping, her eyes shining like maybe—just maybe—she saw me differently now.

Festival of Lights & Laughter

The mehendi, the dance, the aarti—each ritual pulled me deeper into the whirlpool of this wedding.

But nothing prepared me for the festival night—the one that would truly test the current flowing between Aneri and me.

It started with fairy lights strung across the lawn, bonfires crackling in corners, and cousins running around with sparklers. Music floated in the misty Shillong air. The whole place smelled of roasted corn and gulaab jaamoons.

And at the centre of it all was a stage, a microphone, and Aneri—strumming her guitar.

This was no wedding rehearsal. This was magic waiting to happen.

I should have been enjoying it. Instead, I was holding a suspiciously large box of fireworks like it was a ticking bomb.

"Viraaj bhaiya!" one of the kids shouted. "Light this rocket! Show us how it goes!"

Now, here's the thing: I can repair a scooter engine blindfolded. I can rewire a broken mic with chewing gum. But, fireworks? Not my department. Fireworks don't follow logic. They follow chaos.

Still, with ten kids staring at me like I was their captain, I had no choice.

I knelt, stuck the rocket in a bottle, and fumbled with the matchbox.

I struck a match, lit the fuse, and stepped back dramatically.

The rocket hissed, sputtered, and then—
flew sideways.

Straight into the snack counter.

There was a *whoosh*, a shower of sparks, and suddenly jalebees, samosaas, and pakoraas went up like mini fireworks of their own.

Guests screamed. Kids cheered. One uncle shouted, "Arrey, Viraaj, is this new decoration?!"

I flailed, grabbing a bucket of water, dousing the counter until the flames hissed out, leaving behind soggy samosas and jalebees floating like corpses.

The courtyard went silent. Everyone stared at me.

And then—Aneri burst out laughing. Loud, unstoppable, tears-in-her-eyes laughing.

"Oh my god," she gasped. "You just turned the snack counter into *Diwali!*"

I wiped soot off my face, glaring. "This is not funny."

"It's hilarious," she said, still laughing. "Hero of Sangeeth, Slayer of Snacks."

Later, when the chaos calmed and soggy samosaas were replaced, everyone gathered around the main bonfire. The DJ went quiet, and suddenly a soft strum of guitar floated in the air.

Aneri!

She sat near the fire, guitar on her lap, eyes half-closed as she played. The flames painted her in gold. The chatter hushed.

Without thinking, I sat beside her.

"Want me to join?" I asked nervously.

She raised an eyebrow. "With what, your milk bottle as percussion?"

I grinned. "No. With this."

And I started humming. A simple Carnatic alaapana, weaving around her chords. The contrast—her mellow guitar and my raga—was strange at first. But then... it blended.

The bonfire crackled in rhythm. The night seemed to lean closer.

People clapped softly, some swayed. Aneri's voice joined mine, light but firm, carrying the melody higher. And together, we made something neither of us could've alone—a fusion of hills and coasts, ragas and riffs, laughter and longing.

When we finished, silence hung for a moment. Then applause erupted. Cousins whistled, aunties blessed us, uncles demanded encores.

But I wasn't listening.

Because Aneri was looking at me—not smirking, not teasing, just smiling, soft and real.

And I thought: maybe this wasn't just a duet. Maybe this was the beginning of something bigger.

After our bonfire duet, the mood shifted from festive to enchanting. The music lingered in the night air, and for once, nobody rushed, nobody shouted. The fireworks ended in applause, children still jumping and chasing sparks in the smoky air. Music drifted back in, uncles resumed their gossip, aunties returned to their chai.

The lawn sloped gently into the mist. I found myself standing by a half-dead lantern, away from the noise, watching fireflies blink like tiny conspirators in the dark.

"Escaping again?"

I turned. Aneri was walking toward me, guitar slung casually on her back, her face glowing with leftover firelight.

"Not escaping," I said. "Just... catching my breath."

She came to stand beside me, folding her arms. For a moment, neither of us spoke. The mist curled around us like an extra guest.

"You know," she said finally, "you looked terrified holding that sparkler."

"I was," I admitted. "Fire and I... we have had issues."

"And now?" she asked.

I hesitated, then, smiled. "Now... maybe fire and I are on speaking terms."

She chuckled softly, eyes still on the dark hills. "Good. Because fire is... misunderstood. People think it destroys. But sometimes... it just shows you the light."

Her voice dropped, and I caught something raw in it.

"You sound like you've lived that," I said quietly.

She glanced at me, then back at the mist. "When you grow up here, people don't always see *you.* They see stereotypes. They see distance. So yeah... I've had to be fire sometimes. To be seen. To burn away what people think I am."

I swallowed, not sure what to say. Then, softly, I offered, "And did it work?"

She was silent for a long time. Then she whispered, "Some days, yes. Some days... I'm just tired."

The honesty in her voice hit me harder than any firework.

I wanted to tell her I understood. That I knew what it was to be half-nothing, half-everything, to belong everywhere and nowhere.

So, I did.

"I come from two worlds; I have told you that. But, instead of feeling complete, I... just feel split. Never enough."

She turned, really looked at me. And for once, she didn't smirk.

"Maybe," she said softly, "you're not half-and-half, Viraaj. Maybe you are double."

I blinked. "Double?"

"Yeah," she said, smiling faintly. "Two worlds. Two rivers. Twice the stories. Twice the belonging. You're just looking at it wrong."

Her words sat in me like a seed—small, but alive.

We stood there, quiet. The mist wrapped tighter, the distant music muffled, and it felt like the world had shrunk to just this—two people, a dying lantern, and a conversation about fire, fear, and belonging.

Finally, I grinned, breaking the heaviness. "So basically, you're telling me I'm like a double cheese pizza."

She laughed, nudging me with her shoulder. "Exactly. Melty, messy, but impossible to ignore."

I clutched my chest. "Best compliment I've ever received."

She shook her head, still smiling. “Ridiculous.”

And for once, ridiculous felt exactly like destiny.

The Wedding Carnival

If the mehendi was chaos and the sangeeth was war, the next day was... carnival.

The destination wedding had officially taken over Shillong. The resort lawn looked like a mini-fairground: food stalls, game booths, dhol players, even a makeshift photo studio with cardboard cut-outs of Bollywood stars.

"Ring toss! Ring toss!" shouted a cousin.

I was shoved forward. The prize was a giant teddy bear. My target was a row of glass bottles that looked like they had been designed specifically to mock me.

I took the rings, aimed, and missed spectacularly.

The crowd groaned. Aneri, standing nearby, smirked. "Couldn't expect anything better from a journalist."

"Excuse me," I said, adjusting my imaginary tie. "I was a kabaddi champion once."

"Was that before or after you tripped over your own shoelaces?"

Ignoring her, I aimed again, muttering a prayer to all known gods.

The ring sailed—wobbled—clinked—landed. Perfect.

The crowd erupted. The stall owner reluctantly handed me the giant teddy. I staggered under its size, then, handed it to the nearest kid, who cheered like I'd given him a Ferrari.

"Not bad," Aneri admitted, clapping slowly.

We soon got dragged into the Bollywood photo-booth. Cardboard cut-outs of *DDLJ*, *Chennai Express*, *Kabir Singh* (ugh), and *Dil Chahta Hai* lined the backdrop. Props dangled from strings: plastic mandolins, toy guns, sunglasses.

Someone shoved a mandolin into my hand and a chiffon dupatta onto Aneri.

"Arrey, pose like *DDLJ*!" a cousin squealed.

So there we were—me pretending to strum the mandolin, Aneri rolling her eyes holding the dupatta like Simran. The photo was clicked. Everyone cheered.

A cousin zoomed in on the picture. "Wah, kya jodi lag rahi hai!"

We both blushed. Simultaneously muttered, "Shut up."

And then came the big one: the tug of war between the bride's side and the groom's side.

The rope was thick, the ground muddy, and the stakes eternal.

"Viraaj bhaiya! You're captain!" my side shouted.

I froze. "Wait, what? No! I'm not—"

Too late. The whistle blew. The rope tightened.

I dug my heels into the mud, shouting, "One, two, pull!" like a kabaddi raid. The team roared with me. We heaved, strained, slipped and then, suddenly, the other side toppled like dominoes.

Mud splashed everywhere. Kids screamed in joy. My side lifted me onto their shoulders, chanting, "Viraaj! Viraaj!" again.

From the side-lines, Aneri clapped, shaking her head. "You're ridiculous," she mouthed.

And my grin widened. Because ridiculous was winning hearts.

By nightfall, fairy lights twinkled again, music drifted through the mist, and my milk glass clinked against Aneri's chai cup as we sat on the steps, watching the cousins dance.

"You know," she said, smiling sideways, "I think everyone here officially loves you."

"Everyone except the snack counter," I replied.

She laughed, nudging me. "Okay, that one was on you."

And for a moment, everything was perfect.

The music, the laughter, the closeness—it all felt like a dream that could last forever.

But of course, nothing does.

Family Ties

Morning in Shillong smelled like pine trees and masala chai. For everyone else, at least. For me, it smelled like hot milk.

I walked into the courtyard holding my tumbler, bracing for another day of games and gossip. Instead, I found myself surrounded—this time, not by kids or cousins, but by Aneri's *relatives*.

"Aha, our Viraaj beta!" one uncle boomed, clapping me on the back so hard my milk nearly spilled. "Journalist, dancer, mechanic, singer—what else can you do?"

Before I could answer, another aunt chimed in, "He can also handle children! Yesterday, I saw him tie a little one's shoelaces mid-dance rehearsal."

More laughter, more nodding. Someone shouted, "Hero of the snack-counter fire!"

I groaned. "That was an accident."

"Beta," an elder uncle said gravely, "heroes are always accidental. Otherwise, they're politicians."

The crowd erupted in chuckles.

Soon I was dragged to the long breakfast table, which looked more like a buffet than a meal. Plates of idlis, aaloo paraathaas, momos, poha—it was like every state of India had sent a food ambassador.

"Viraaj, come sit here!" one aunty beckoned. "Eat, beta, eat!"

I sat, already sweating at the sight of so much food.

"Paraathaa?" someone asked.

"Yes, please."

"Idli?"

"Yes, sure."

"Momo?"

"...Okay."

Within minutes, my plate was a mini-mountain. Aneri slid into the seat across from me, smirking.

"Careful," she whispered. "They're testing you."

"Testing me?" I mouthed.

"Yes. If you eat everything, you're polite. If you refuse anything, you're arrogant."

I stared at the pile on my plate. "So this is... an exam?"

"Yup," she grinned. "Food IAS."

So I did what any brave man would do—I ate. Idli dunked in chutney, paraathaa dripping ghee, momos burning my tongue, poha sweet and spicy all at once. My stomach screamed for mercy, but I soldiered on.

By the end, I leaned back, dazed, my plate empty. The aunties applauded.

"Wah, Viraaj beta! He eats like family!"

I raised a weak fist in triumph. Aneri nearly fell off her chair laughing.

After the feast I found myself sitting in a circle of elders, listening to them tell stories about Shillong in the old days—markets, music festivals, long walks in the rain. They looked surprised when I leaned forward, genuinely curious, asking questions, scribbling notes in my little reporter's pad.

"You really listen, beta," one uncle said. "Not like these phone-scrolling children."

"Listening is my job," I said with a smile. "But also... your stories are too good to waste."

And just like that, they started warming up. By the time the afternoon rolled in, I was no longer "the bride's cousin."

I was "Viraaj beta."

Across the courtyard, Aneri leaned against the balcony railing, watching it all unfold—I laughing with the uncles, helping the aunties carry trays, playing kabaddi with the kids in the garden.

One cousin nudged her, teasing, "Arrey Aneri, your friend from Chennai is stealing all our hearts."

She rolled her eyes, but she was smiling.

Later, when we crossed paths near the staircase, she whispered, "Careful. Another day like this, and they'll start calling you *ghar ka ladka.*"

"Would that be so bad?" I teased.

She opened her mouth, then, shut it. Her smile faded into something softer. "Maybe not," she murmured.

For a moment, we just stood there, caught in a silence that said more than words could.

And that was when I realized—
I wasn't just winning over the family.
I was slipping quietly, dangerously, into their daughter's heart too.

The Shillong Fair

The next morning, the whole wedding gang packed into jeeps for a "family outing." Apparently, when people plan destination weddings in Shillong, they don't just do rituals—they do tourism too.

Our convoy wound through pine forests, past waterfalls draped like silver scarves, until we reached the local fairground.

It was magic—rows of stalls glowing with collared bulbs, the smell of roasted corn and bamboo shoots in the air, giant wheels turning lazily against the blue sky.

The kids bolted immediately. The aunties fanned themselves dramatically. The uncles compared prices of sugarcane juice like it was the stock market.

And, me? I was dragged straight into the chaos again.

"Viraaj bhaiya! Shoot the balloons!" the kids demanded.

I picked up the toy rifle, squinted at the line of rainbow balloons, and fired. *Pop!* First try. Then, another. Then, another.

The stall-owner's jaw dropped.

The kids erupted. "Wah bhaiya! Sniper!"

Someone even shouted, "JOURNALIST JAMES BOND!"

Across the crowd, Aneri whistled and clapped slowly. "Impressive, Milkman. I didn't know you had aim."

I grinned, handing her the rifle. "Your turn."

She raised it, fired—and popped two balloons at once.

The kids went wild. I stared, stunned.

"Beginner's luck," she shrugged, smirking.

"Or maybe you're secretly Wonder Woman," I muttered.

She laughed. "Don't flatter me, you'll get addicted."

Later, a group of cousins pushed us toward the giant wheel.

"Couples only, bhaiya!" the operator said firmly, shoving people into pairs.

Before I could protest, I found myself squeezed into a creaky seat beside Aneri, the wheel already lifting us into the sky.

"Perfect," she said dryly. "Trapped with you."

"Hey, I'm excellent company," I said. "I can list five fun milk facts."

"Please don't."

We rose higher, the fair shrinking below us, the hills spreading out in misty waves. For a moment, there was silence.

Then Aneri whispered, almost to herself, "Beautiful isn't it?"

I looked at the view. Then, at her.

"Yes," I said softly. "Beautiful."

She turned, caught me staring, and rolled her eyes—but her cheeks flushed pink in the chilly air.

On the way back, we passed a fortune-teller's tent. A colourful banner screamed *"Know your destiny in 5 minutes!"*

Cousins shoved us inside. The old woman inside peered at my palm, nodding gravely.

"You," she said. "You are… fire and water. Two halves, always restless."

Aneri raised an eyebrow. "Sounds accurate."

The woman turned to her. "And you. You are flame hidden in mist. Stronger than you believe."

Then she looked at both of us together. "Your paths… they are tangled. Not simple. But light is there, if you hold on."

We froze. The cousins giggled outside, shouting, "Shaadi prediction!"

We stumbled out, embarrassed, but something about her words stuck in me. Tangled paths. Light, if we held on.

By evening, the families loaded back into jeeps, laughing, carrying bags of toys and snacks. I sat by the window, watching the hills blur past, my hand brushing against Aneri's when the jeep jolted.

Neither of us pulled away.

And as the sky turned gold and the day folded into memory, I thought—
if destiny had a taste, it would taste like roasted corn and laughter in the Shillong mist.

But of course, destiny wasn't finished with us yet.

Just when I thought I'd survived the fair—balloon-shooting, Ferris wheel, fortune-teller—a cousin spotted a food stall.

"Bhaiya!" he shouted. "Eat-off challenge! You have to try!"

The crowd dragged me to a bamboo shack where a board proudly declared:

"SPICY KING CHALLENGE!
10 MOMOS IN 5 MINUTES!
WITH OUR SPECIAL CHUTNEY.
WINNERS GET FREE DINNER VOUCHER!"

Aneri's eyes lit up with mischief. "Oh, this is perfect. Milkman versus momos."

"Absolutely not," I said, backing away. "You saw what one chutney did to me yesterday."

She smirked. "Scared?"

I straightened. "I'm not scared. I'm... respectful of my digestive system."

"Translation: scared," she said, folding her arms.

The cousins started chanting, "Viraaj! Viraaj!" The stall-owner banged a spoon against a plate like a referee.

And just like that, I was seated at the table, ten steaming momos in front of me, and a bowl of chutney that looked like liquid lava and a timer ready.

The whistle blew. I picked up the first momo, dunked it into chutney, and shoved it into my mouth.

Instant fire! My tongue screamed, my eyes watered, my ears rang.

The cousins howled with laughter. Aneri doubled over, clutching her stomach.

"Come on, Milkman!" she shouted between giggles. "Don't let the chutney defeat you!"

I soldiered on. Second momo. Third. By the fourth, my face was crimson, my nose running, and my shirt damp with sweat. I gulped milk between bites like it was holy water.

The crowd chanted louder. "Bhaiya! Bhaiya!"

By the seventh momo, I was hallucinating. I saw Lord Ganesha dancing to "Deva Shree Ganesha" in the chutney bowl. By the eighth, I was bargaining with the universe.

Finally, with a roar that came out more like a whimper, I shoved the tenth momo in. The whistle blew.

The crowd erupted. The stall-owner raised my arm like I'd won a boxing match. "Champion!"

I staggered to my feet, wiping sweat. My stomach felt like a battlefield. Aneri appeared, still laughing, holding out a glass of cold milk.

"Here," she said her voice gentler now. "You earned it."

I took it, gulped it down, and gasped. "This... this is why milk is the elixir of life."

She shook her head, grinning. "You're ridiculous. But impressive. I didn't think you'd last past three."

I gave her a weak bow. "Never underestimate a Milkman with a cause."

And just like that, the cousins hoisted me onto their shoulders again, chanting, "Viraaj! Viraaj!" while Aneri clapped, laughing, her eyes sparkling in a way that made all the spice worth it.

By the time we left the fair, my stomach had forgiven me, the cousins had declared me their "Momo King," and Aneri... well, and she looked at me with that same half-smile she always wore when I surprised her.

The jeep ride back was quiet, but our shoulders brushed the whole way. Neither of us moved.

And as the lights of Shillong flickered in the distance, I thought:

If this was the carnival before the storm, then I never wanted the storm to come.

But storms don't ask.

They arrive.

The fair had ended, the kids were asleep, the aunties exhausted, and the uncles slightly tipsy on whatever "herbal tonic" they'd smuggled in.

The resort was quiet now, fairy lights swaying in the mist, the distant hills glowing faintly under the moon.

I stepped out onto the terrace of my room with my faithful tumbler of milk. The cool air hit my face, carrying the faint scent of pine and fried snacks. My stomach still grumbled from the momo massacre, but my heart... my heart felt oddly light.

That's when I heard it.

A faint strumming.

I leaned over the railing. Down in the courtyard, on a wooden bench, sat Aneri with her guitar. Barefoot, hair loose, singing softly to herself. Not for an audience this time. Just... for the night.

I crept down quietly, milk in hand, and sat on the bench opposite her. She didn't stop singing, just raised an eyebrow at me mid-verse.

"Don't you ever sleep?" she asked after finishing the song.

"Journalists don't sleep," I said. "We collect stories at night."

"And what's tonight's story?"

I held up the tumbler. "Boy drinks milk. Girl sings under the moon. World doesn't notice, but the boy does."

She snorted, shaking her head. "Cheesy."

"Hey," I said, grinning. "I'm half Banaarasi by blood. We live for cheesy shaayari."

I cleared my throat and improvised:

"Chaand ke neechey tu guitar bajaaye,
Doodh pi ke sher ban jaaye,
Duniya hansi, par kya farq hai—
Tu yahaan hai, bas yahi pyaar hai."

She laughed so hard she almost dropped her guitar. "Oh my god, that's terrible!"

"Thank you," I said proudly.

Her laughter softened into a smile. "You know... you're the first person I've met in a long time who doesn't try to impress me. You just... are. Clumsy, silly, ridiculous—but real."

I blinked, caught off-guard. "That's... good, right?"

She nodded, looking down at her strings. "It's... rare."

The silence that followed wasn't empty. It was full—of sparks, of unspoken things, of the kind of weight you don't feel until it's there.

Finally, she looked up. "Viraaj... do you ever think maybe... destiny isn't about where you're from, but who you meet?"

I stared at her, my chest tightening. "I think destiny is... sitting on this bench, drinking milk, listening to you sing."

She rolled her eyes at my filmy answer, but her smile lingered.

We sat there a while longer, her guitar humming softly, my tumbler warming my hands, the mist curling around us like a secret.

And in that quiet, I felt it—something beyond fun, beyond banter, beyond accident.

Something dangerously close to love.

The courtyard had emptied into silence. Even the fairy lights seemed drowsy, flickering lazily in the mist. Aneri strummed a few gentle chords; her voice humming like the hills themselves had leaned in to listen.

I sat opposite her, holding my tumbler of milk, but not drinking. My eyes were on her, the way the firelight of the lantern touched her hair, the way her fingers moved on the strings.

"You know," I said softly, "if you keep playing like this, I'll start believing life is actually a film."

She looked up, amused. “And which one would it be?”

“Easy,” I said. “A Shahrukh Khan movie. Where the hero is clumsy, ridiculous, but somehow ends up with the girl.”

She chuckled, shaking her head. “You and your SRK obsession.”

“Hey,” I protested. “SRK raised an entire generation of men who don’t know how to fight but know how to love. I’m one of them.”

Her smile softened. She stopped strumming, just holding the guitar still on her lap. The night thickened between us.

“Viraaj,” she said quietly, “you ever think about... what this is?”

My heart thudded. “This?”

“You and me,” she said, meeting my eyes. “The way we’ve been... since the train. Since the mehendi, the sangeeth, the fair.”

I swallowed, words tumbling to the edge of my tongue. “Aneri... I—”

But before I could say it, a door croaked open nearby. A gaggle of cousins spilled out, laughing, one of them shouting, “Arrey, what are you two doing here, haan? Secret meeting?”

We sprang apart, guilty as teenagers. Aneri’s cheeks flushed pink, her smile returning in a quick mask.

I raised my tumbler. “Milk party,” I said lamely.

The cousins hooted. “Milk party! Wah wah! Love story ka new code word!”

Aneri rolled her eyes, shooing them away. But the moment was gone—the delicate thread of honesty snapped by laughter and noise.

She stood, brushing her hair back. "We should... sleep. Big day tomorrow."

I wanted to stop her. To finish what I almost said. To tell her she was more than a train coincidence, more than a sparkler partner, more than just funny banter in the night.

But all I managed was: "Yeah. Big day."

She gave me one last look—half-smile, half-something else—and walked back toward her room.

I sat there a while longer, alone with my milk and my almost-confession, staring at the mist curling through the resort.

And that's when I felt it. The shift.

The kind of silence that isn't calm, but a warning.

The storm was coming.

The Suitor Appears

The haldi was chaos.

And not the usual chaos of turmeric-paste smearing and cousins running amok. No, this was next-level chaos. Because it wasn't just *a* wedding anymore.

It was our cousins' wedding.
Aneri's cousin was the groom.
My cousin was the bride.
Same wedding. Same stage. Same families colliding like two trains on one track.

So, the courtyard was a battlefield: aunties from Banaras arguing with others about whether turmeric should be mixed with rose water or coconut oil, while aunties from Shillong clicked their tongues and added herbs none of us could pronounce. Meanwhile, the bride's side tried to smear the groom with haldi paste, the groom's side fought back, and somehow I ended up with a giant yellow handprint across my cheek.

"Looking good, Milkman," Aneri teased, holding a bowl of haldi like a weapon.

"Don't even think about it," I warned.

Too late. She smeared a streak across my arm, laughing like a maniac. I retaliated with a splash, missed her entirely, and hit her cousin's dog instead. The poor thing looked like a jaundiced lion.

Everyone roared with laughter, and for a moment, I forgot the tension building in the background.

Because *he* had arrived.

I first noticed him by the way the crowd shifted. Elders suddenly stood straighter. Aunties smoothed their saarees. Aneri's father lit up with a smile wider than I'd ever seen on him.

And then, there he was.

Rishav Jyrwa.

Polished kurta. Designer watch glinting in the sunlight with a smile like he had practiced it in a mirror -.the kind of man who spoke as though the world had been built for his approval.

He walked in like he owned the place. Hugged Aneri's uncle. Touched her grandmother's feet. Shook hands with her father like a politician sealing a deal.

And when his eyes finally landed on me, they sharpened. Just slightly. Enough for me to feel the prickle.

"Who's that?" he asked loudly enough for half the courtyard to hear.

"Ah, Viraaj," Aneri's father said with a smile. "The groom's cousin. From Chennai. A journalist."

Rishav smirked, his handshake firm, almost crushing. "Journalist, huh? Cute hobby."

"Pays the bills," I said, forcing a grin.

He tilted his head, sizing me up. "If the bills are small."

Laughter rippled through the uncles nearby. My ears burned.

Aneri, to her credit, stepped in quickly. "This is Viraaj. He's family. And he's... helpful."

Helpful. Like a friendly Labrador.

Great.

That evening, both families gathered for a massive dinner spread. Plates of idlis, trays of litti-chokha, steaming momos, and fish curry sat side by side like the United Nations of cuisine.

I sat at the far end, trying to survive aunties piling food on my plate like they were trying to fatten me for a sacrifice.

And then Rishav sat across from me.

"So, Viraaj," he said smoothly, scooping biryani. "You must be very busy. Covering... traffic jams? Celebrity gossip?"

"I cover stories that matter," I said. "Like housing rights, corruption, missing voices."

He smirked. "Noble. But where does that get you in ten years?"

I opened my mouth, but Aneri's cousin interrupted with laughter. "Viraaj bhaiya! Tell him how you only drink milk!"

Rishav raised an eyebrow. "Milk?"

"Yep," Aneri said cheerfully, though I noticed the edge in her smile. "He hates chai. Can't stand coffee. He's a milk guy."

The table erupted in chuckles. Rishav leaned back, smirking. "Figures."

Something inside me clenched.

Later, when the laughter had died and people drifted away, I found myself on the balcony with my tumbler of milk. The stars felt like they were judging me too.

Aneri slipped out beside me, arms folded.

"You're sulking," she said.

"I'm not sulking."

"You're absolutely sulking."

I sighed. "He's perfect, isn't he? Tall, rich, connected. Knows everyone. Your family loves him. Meanwhile, I'm just... half this, half that. Milk-drinker journalist. Nothing special."

She frowned, leaning against the railing. "You think that's what I care about?"

"It's what they care about."

Her voice softened. "Maybe. But I'm not them."

I looked at her. She met my eyes steadily, a tiny smile tugging her lips.

"You're not half-anything, Viraaj. You're double. Double the stories, double the cultures, double the chaos. That's why..." She stopped herself, looked away. "That's why you matter."

The silence stretched. My heart pounded.

And then, inside the hall, someone called her name. She sighed, straightened. "Don't let him get to you, Milkman. He's not as perfect as he looks."

I watched her go, the warmth of her words clashing with the sting of Rishav's smirk.

For the first time since the train, I wondered if destiny had made a mistake.

The next morning, the temple festival began.

Drums thundered. Stalls overflowed with sweets. Kids darted between legs with sparklers. The air was alive with laughter.

But in the shadows of the market, Rishav's men watched me.

And I knew — this wasn't just a wedding anymore.

It was a battlefield.

Festival Fallout, Bridges, and Cracks

The Shillong temple festival was an explosion of colour.

The courtyard was lit with paper lanterns strung between pine trees. The air smelled of steaming momos, litti-chokha, and jalebees. Drums thundered near the temple steps. Kids darted with sparklers while elders argued about puja timings.

And in the middle of all this madness, I—Viraaj Naraen—was clutching my tumbler of milk and trying not to trip over a kite string.

That's when I noticed them.

Three men, standing too still in a moving crowd. Rishav's men.

"Viraaj?" one of them barked.

I forced a smile. "Depends. If this is about the time I spilled chutney on your boss's shoe—"

Irritated, they lunged.

I bolted through the festival lane, nearly knocking over a momo stall. Dumplings flew like grenades. The crowd roared with laughter, assuming it was some street performance.

My foot slipped on spilled chutney, and I crashed into a paani puri (water pancakes) cart. Golgappas (water pancakes) exploded like shrapnel. The band wallaahs, thinking it part of the show, struck up an even louder tune.

I spotted an abandoned scooter leaning against a pole, wires dangling like a patient on life support. Without thinking, my hands moved—green thumb instinct. Spark plug, ignition wire, one swift kick.

The scooter roared to life and shot forward... without me.

Straight into the goons.

They toppled like bowling pins into a pile of firecrackers.

BOOM-BOOM-BOOM.

The sky lit with sparks. Kids screamed with delight. Aunties clutched their saarees. And there I stood, panting, clutching my milk like a sword.

"Viraaj!"

I turned. Aneri was rushing toward me, dupatta flying, bamboo stick in hand. One half-dazed goon tried to rise—she smacked his shin so hard he howled and limped away.

I gaped. "You—what—"

"Saved you. Again," she said, eyes blazing.

We ran through the laughter, sparks, and drums until we collapsed behind the temple steps, breathless and smeared in chutney.

"You're insane," she laughed.

"I fixed a scooter mid-chase," I wheezed.

"You also almost got killed."

"Details," I said.

She shook her head, but her smile lingered. And for a heartbeat, sitting there beside her, I didn't feel like half-anything.

I felt whole.

That night, the wedding resort buzzed with rumours— "Viraaj staged a stunt," "the gods blessed him," "the new boy's luck."

I slipped to the balcony; phone pressed to my ear.

"Pa?"

My father's calm, railway-official voice came on. "Viraaj. You sound tired."

"Just... festival chaos." I tried to laugh, but it cracked.

Silence. Then: "What is it, son? Tell me."

I hesitated. "It's just... there's someone new. Everyone admires him. Perfect family, perfect image. And me—I want to be accepted, Pa. But it feels... impossible."

My father didn't answer immediately. Then he spoke, measured as always.

"Viraaj, do you remember your Carnatic teacher? How he made you sing one single note for hours until your voice trembled?"

"Yes," I muttered.

"That note—again and again—was not punishment. It was discipline. Perseverance. You are not half-anything. You are train and river. Discipline and laughter. That is your strength. Sing your note, son. The world will adjust to your pitch."

I swallowed, throat burning. "Pa..."

Then Mumma's voice came, gentle but firm. "Beta, you've always wanted everyone to love you. But not everyone will. That is the truth of life. Don't waste yourself chasing their approval. Stand by the ones who see you truly. That is where your courage lives."

Her words cut deep, simple and unshakable.

"Mumma," I whispered, "thank you."

She laughed softly. "Don't thank us. Just remember—bridges aren't built in one day. Keep laying stones."

I stood there, phone pressed tight, eyes stinging, knowing they couldn't see my tears—but somehow sensing they knew anyway.

Aneri's Cracks

My father didn't even mention Viraaj. Not once.

To him, Viraaj wasn't even in the picture. Invisible.

Instead, he praised Rishav all evening to the relatives—his connections, his polished manners, his family's influence. My mother nodded quietly, as she always did, though her eyes flickered with worry.

But I heard the snide comments from others.

I smiled politely through it, as though the words bounced off. But inside, they burned.

Because when I closed my eyes, I didn't see Rishav in his perfect kurta. I saw Viraaj at the festival—face flushed, chutney-stained, fixing a scooter like a magician, clutching his milk tumbler like a sword.

And I remembered his laughter, his absurd courage, his voice when he'd joked, Details.

They saw him as a joke. I saw him as... more.

And though I sat there nodding as my father talked of Rishav, a quiet rebellion bloomed inside me.

I wasn't sure how much longer I could keep smiling.

But I knew one thing:

I was already dreaming of Viraaj.

Songs in the Mist

Nights in Shillong are deceptive.

The mist doesn't just roll in; it sneaks up on you, veiling the lights of the resort until you feel like you're sitting in a dream you can't quite trust.

I found myself in the courtyard long after everyone had gone to bed. The haldi and sangeeth chaos had ended, aunties had passed out in their saarees, and uncles were snoring in chorus. Even the bride—my cousin Riya—was locked away with her mother fussing over final jewellery lists.

I sat with my tumbler of milk, staring at the lamps glowing through mist. For once, it felt like the world had pressed pause.

And then I heard it.

A guitar.

Soft, unhurried chords slicing the silence like warm butter.

I turned, and there she was—Aneri. Sitting on the steps, her acoustic guitar balanced on her lap, strumming like it was the most natural thing in the world.

I don't know why, but I stopped breathing.

She looked up and saw me. Instead of stopping, she smiled. "Well? Don't just stare. Come sit."

I sat a little awkwardly, milk tumbler sweating in my hands.

"What are you playing?" I asked.

"Something unfinished," she said. "A song that refuses to end. Like Shillong mist."

I nodded, unsure.

"Sing with me," she said suddenly.

I nearly choked. "What? No. I... I don't—"

"Oh please," she rolled her eyes. "You're the Carnatic boy. I've heard you. Don't pretend."

I swallowed. She wasn't wrong. Years of my father's discipline, mornings of shruti box droning, my mother's poetry filling lyrics. I could sing. But I'd never thought it mattered outside small sabhas in Chennai.

Still, something about the mist, her guitar, the way her eyes dared me—I opened my mouth.

And sang.

A simple raga. A note rising and falling, threading through her chords.

She matched me, her strums bending to the melody. My voice soared higher, then dipped, and her guitar wrapped around it like a lover's arm. She started humming, then singing, and suddenly we were weaving something neither of us had planned.

Carnatic ragas met acoustic strings. Hills met rivers.

We weren't perfect, but we were real.

When we stopped, breathless, there was silence.

Then—claps.

We turned. A cluster of cousins had gathered in the mist, wide-eyed. Riya, my bride-cousin, stood among them, hands pressed to her mouth, eyes shining.

"That was..." she whispered, "beautiful."

Another cousin yelled, "Encore!"

Before I could protest, Aneri grinned, strummed again, and pulled me into another tune. This time, we laughed between lines, stumbling but not caring. The cousins joined, clapping in rhythm, the mist glowing with sound.

By the time we ended, everyone was smiling like children.

"Good night, superstars!" one cousin teased as they drifted off.

I sank back, embarrassed but buzzing. Aneri looked at me, eyes soft.

“See, Milkman?” she whispered. “You’re not half-anything. You’re whole. Always were.”

I couldn’t reply. My throat was too full—with mist, with music, with her.

When it was just us again, silence stretched.

I wanted to say it. The words. The truth.

But instead, I blurted, “Your guitar’s out of tune on the B string.”

She laughed so hard she almost dropped it. “You’re hopeless.”

But her smile lingered, and for a second, I thought—maybe she’d understood anyway.

Pressure Mounts

The morning after our duet in the mist, I woke to the sound of wedding drums.

Not unusual. The whole resort had been vibrating with dhols since I got here. But this beat felt heavier. Urgent.

By the time I reached the courtyard, I knew why.

It wasn't just wedding prep. It was politics disguised as family duty.

Amid the colours, Rishav appeared.

Not as a guest this time. But, as a centre.

A priest had been called. A table set with flowers. And her father—Mr. Dhar, government official, authoritative voice, eyes sharp as law—was standing with Rishav's family.

Aneri stood frozen near her mother; the only obvious sign of rebellion was visible in the stiffness of her jaw.

I didn't need an announcement. I already knew.

An "informal engagement."

Dress rehearsal for a future they had already decided.

I stood near the back with my mother's side of the family.

Prashaant Maama and Varuna Maami—my bride-cousin's parents—offered me supportive smiles, but the other Raghuvanshi relatives whispered.

"Viraaj Naraen? What does he do again? Journalism?"
"Ah yes, stand-up too. Funny boy. But what future is that?"
"Mixed roots too."

Their words stung sharper than I let show. I kept my face neutral, but inside, I burned.

Because, at that moment, I wasn't even on the stage. I wasn't even in the frame.

I was background.

From where I stood, I saw her father's hand on her shoulder, steering her forward. Her mother's nervous glances and Rishav's smug smile as the priest recited lines about auspicious beginnings was something that everyone noticed."

Aneri didn't smile. She didn't nod. She didn't move.

But she didn't refuse either.

I wanted to storm forward. Grab her hand. Pull her away.

But Pa's voice from last night echoed: *"Sing your note, son. Again and again, until the world adjusts to your pitch."*

So I stayed still. Watching. Waiting.

When the priest asked her to place a garland on Rishav, the silence was deafening.

She looked at the flowers. Looked at Rishav. Looked at her father.

Then she spoke, voice low but cutting.

"Not yet. It's my cousin's wedding. Let's not steal their stage."

Polite. Calm. But unyielding.

Her father frowned, but nodded. Rishav's jaw tightened, though he masked it with another plastic smile. The garland was set aside. The priest dismissed.

The crisis postponed. Not ended.

But Aneri's eyes flickered toward me in the crowd. Just once. Just long enough for me to see it—fear, yes. But also defiance.

That night, I found her alone on the balcony, guitar resting beside her.

"You stopped it," I said softly.

She shrugged. "Delayed it."

"That's still something."

She turned, her eyes shining with unshed frustration. "They don't even see me, Viraaj. To them, I'm just... an extension of the family. A pawn in their games."

I stepped closer. "You're not a pawn. You're—" I stopped. Words jammed in my throat.

She raised an eyebrow. "I'm...?"

I smiled faintly. "A queen. Who plays the guitar better than anyone I've ever met"?

Her laugh broke the tension. Short, sharp, real.

"Viraaj," she said, quieter now. "Do you ever feel like... you're fighting an invisible battle? Everyone else has rules and boxes, and you're... just trying to exist?"

"All the time," I said. "People don't know where to slot me, so they just... don't."

She looked at me, something soft breaking through her exhaustion. "And how do you survive it?"

I thought of Pa's voice. Mumma's words. My grandfather's laughter over cricket.

"By laughing," I said. "By writing. By being stubborn. By knowing that if I can make even one person see me... it's enough."

Her lips parted, as though to speak, but she just nodded, looking away.

We stood in silence. The mist curled around us, thick as truth.

And I knew—pressure was building. The engagement hadn't gone. Just waiting in the shadows.

But so was I.

Comedy as Courage

The sangeeth after-party was supposed to be simple.

A small gathering after the grand performances, with cousins cracking jokes, maybe someone singing, and people gossiping about who had danced worst.

Instead, it became my stage.

"Viraaj beta," Varuna Maami cornered me with a smile. "You're the only one with stage presence. Host the after-party. Make everyone laugh."

I froze. "Me?"

"Yes, you," she said firmly. "You're the journalist and stand-up comedian, na? Use your words. Turn this tension into laughter."

I knew what she meant. The air was thick—Aneri's family pushing their agenda, Rishav strutting around like a prize stallion, my own relatives muttering doubts about me. The room needed laughter.

And suddenly, I realized—I needed it too.

I walked up, grabbed the mic my hands trembled, but the moment I looked at the crowd, instinct took over.

"Good evening, ladies, gentlemen, and politicians pretending to be gentlemen."

Laughter. A ripple. Good start.

"You know, weddings are magical. Two families come together. In this case, Raghuvanshis from Banaras and Mukhims from Shillong. A perfect union. Until someone remembers politics. Then suddenly it's less 'shaadi' and more 'Rajya Sabha session.'"

More laughter. Heads turned toward the Mukhim elders. Even they chuckled uneasily.

I leaned forward. "But seriously—politics in India is fascinating. Before elections: 'Hum gareebon ke liye jeeyenge.' (We will live for the poor) After elections: 'Gareeb? Who?'" (Poor? Who?)

The crowd roared.

Rishav shifted uncomfortably.

I grinned, voice sharper now. "And then we have the polished types. The ones who smile perfectly, shake hands perfectly, touch feet perfectly. But inside?" I tapped the mic. "They see people not as humans, but as trophies. Connections. Political mileage. Like Pokémon cards. Collect 'em all!"

Gasps. Laughter. Some elders frowned, but the younger cousins howled.

"And you know the saddest part? These people deserve our sympathy. Truly. Because imagine never learning empathy. Never learning brotherhood. Never learning to see beyond your own shelf of prizes. If you can't even understand yourself, what good will you do for others?"

The hall fell silent for a beat. Then, applause. Loud, spontaneous.

Even Riya clapped, eyes shining with pride.

I caught Aneri's gaze. She wasn't laughing—she was glowing.

I ended softer. "But weddings teach us something politics never does. Brotherhood. Empathy. Love. You don't need power to unite families—you just need music, dance, food… and a lot of turmeric."

The hall erupted.

I bowed, handed the mic back, and slipped off stage.

People slapped my back, laughing. "Arrey, Viraaj, you're too much!" "Beta, that was bold!" "Sharp tongue, haan?"

Rishav didn't laugh. His jaw was tight, smile thin.

But Aneri found me later, guitar slung across her back.

"That was brave," she said softly. "Dangerously brave."

I shrugged. "Just… my note. Sung loudly."

Her smile was small, but her eyes—her eyes said everything.

The laughter of the crowd still echoed in my ears as people drifted away.

Uncles chuckled, patting my back. "Beta, that was brave!"
Aunties shook their heads, half-scolding, half-proud. "Your tongue will get you in trouble, Viraaj."
Riya beamed at me, whispering, "That's my cousin!"

But I noticed him.

Mr. Dhar. Aneri's Father.

Tall, dignified, his kurta crisp, his gaze steady as a river. He hadn't laughed. He hadn't frowned. He'd only watched.

And now, as the hall emptied, his voice cut through the air.

"Viraaj Naraen. A word."

We stood in a quieter corridor, away from the chatter. Aneri lingered at a distance, almost hidden in the shadows, her guitar slung casually but her eyes sharp, as though ready to leap in if things went wrong.

Her father folded his arms. "You speak boldly. Too boldly. Do you think jokes can fix this country?"

I steadied my voice. "No, sir. But jokes can open ears that refuse lectures. Words can slip past defences when anger cannot."

He raised an eyebrow. "You're a journalist. A stand-up comedian. Is that how you see politics? As a circus?"

I swallowed, then, shook my head. "No, sir. I see politics as a stage. The problem is that too many actors have forgotten the script — serving people. And, the youth? We've been told to sit in the audience, clap or jeer, but never step up."

His gaze sharpened. "And you think youth can do better?"

"Yes," I said, louder now. "Because we don't see caste or creed first — we see problems. Jobs. Schools. Hospitals. Because we know empathy isn't weakness. It's strength. Because we're tired of being told our voices don't matter."

For a long moment, he said nothing. Then his voice softened, but only slightly.

"Young men speak of ideals. But governance is not ideals. It is compromise. Sacrifice. Do you understand that?"

I met his gaze. "I do, sir. My father works in Railways. Every day he keeps trains running through floods, strikes, and chaos. My mother writes—she uses words to heal. They taught me compromise is necessary, yes. But silence?" I shook my head. "Silence kills."

His eyes flickered. Something shifted.

"And you," he pressed, "think words are enough?"

"Not alone," I admitted. "But words are where it begins. A headline sparks thought. A joke sparks reflection. A poem sparks empathy. And if one person changes, maybe ten more will. That's how revolutions start—not with bombs, but with whispers loud enough to become shouts."

I didn't know she was holding her breath, but Aneri was.

From where she stood, she saw her father's posture ease, just slightly. His eyes, usually sharp, softened. He wasn't convinced, not yet — but he was listening.

She had prepared to step in, to save me from scolding. Instead, she watched something she'd never seen: her father in real dialogue, not with a minister or party member, but with someone who believed enough to challenge him without disrespect.

She realized then—Viraaj wasn't just witty. He wasn't just brave. He was dangerous in the best way. Because, he believed.

Finally, Mr. Dhar exhaled, long and measured.

"You speak well, Viraaj. Perhaps, too well."

I held my breath.

Then he said quietly, "This country... needs more youth like you. Who care enough to speak, even when no one listens."

My chest tightened. I bowed slightly. "Thank you, sir."

He gave a brief nod, then walked away, leaving me stunned in the corridor.

When I turned, Aneri was there, smiling faintly.

"You just debated my father," she whispered.

"I survived?" I asked weakly.

"More than survived," she said. "You made him think. Trust me—that's rare."

Her hand brushed mine for a second before she walked past. Just a brush. But, enough to make my heart race louder than the drums.

And for the first time, I thought: maybe, just maybe, I wasn't fighting alone.

The corridor emptied. The sound of dhols faded behind closed doors.

Mr. Dhar stood alone, his back to the lanterns, looking out at the mist curling over the hills. For the first time since I'd met him, his posture wasn't that of an official, but of a man weighed down.

Unaware, I lingered near the corner. Aneri lingered too, silent as a shadow.

He spoke softly, almost to himself.

"Youth," he muttered. "Always, so certain. So sure the world bends to will. I was like that once. Before politics. Before files and compromises."

He exhaled, slow. "But that boy... he speaks not for himself. He speaks like someone who has seen both sides of the country. Railway dust and poetry. Maybe... maybe we do need more like him."

The words weren't an admission, not fully. But they were more than silence.

Aneri's throat tightened. Her father, the immovable mountain, had shifted—if only by a pebble.

The groom's parents walked in.

"Bah Ba," a voice called gently. The mist parted to reveal two figures—her uncle, Ranjit Dhar (the groom's father, younger brother of Mr. Dhar), and his wife, Neena Mukhim.

They approached slowly, as though they had heard part of the conversation.

"Elder brother," Ranjit said softly, "you look thoughtful."

Mr. Dhar straightened, mask returning. "Nothing. Just... reflections."

But Neena glanced at him knowingly before turning to her husband. "That Viraaj... he's unusual."

"Yes," Ranjit agreed. "Too outspoken for his own good." He paused. "But brave."

Their words made me shift nervously. Aneri, hidden behind a pillar, caught her breath.

Mr. Dhar's expression didn't change, but his silence wasn't dismissive. For once, it was contemplative.

Ranjit chuckled softly. "In our family, Bah Ba, we've always been afraid of boys who laugh too much. We forget that laughter can be a kind of courage."

Neena added gently, "And he sang last night, didn't he? With Aneri. I saw them. The cousins said it was... magical."

A flicker crossed Mr. Dhar's face. He didn't answer, but the air between the three felt alive with unspoken debate.

From the shadows, Aneri's chest ached with something she couldn't name. Pride. Fear. Hope.

Her father wasn't convinced. Not yet. But for the first time, he hadn't dismissed Viraaj outright.

And her uncle and aunt—the younger Dhars—were watching too, not with hostility, but with curiosity.

Maybe, just maybe, Viraaj wasn't alone anymore.

The Younger Dhars' Curiosity

The festival laughter had died down. The resort halls buzzed with last-minute rehearsals, the smell of pine and incense heavy in the air.

I had just slipped into the veranda for air when I heard a voice.

"Viraaj, beta?"

I turned. Standing there were Ranjit Dhar and Neena Mukhim—the groom's parents. Aneri's uncle and aunt.

The younger brother of Mr. Dhar didn't carry the same stiff authority. He had softer edges in his voice, but his eyes were just as sharp. Neena stood beside him, graceful, watchful.

"Ji, Uncle?" I asked politely.

"Walk with us," Ranjit said. Not a request.

We strolled along the garden path, lanterns swaying in the mist. Neena broke the silence first.

"You spoke boldly tonight."

I smiled faintly. "Too boldly, maybe."

Ranjit glanced at me. "Boldness can be dangerous. But, also useful. Do you always speak like this?"

I hesitated. "Only when I feel silence would be worse."

Neena studied me. "You're a journalist, na?"

"Yes, ma'am. I did my Master's in Journalism. Words... they're my way of fighting. Word by word, story by story."

Ranjit raised an eyebrow. "And comedy?"

I chuckled softly. "Comedy is my way of healing. The country laughs at its own wounds, and somehow, laughter makes them lighter. Politicians don't know whether to love me or hate me."

That made Neena laugh quietly, surprising me. "And, your family? What do they say about this?"

"My father works in the Railways," I said. "He believes in discipline, trains running on time, no excuses. My mother—she's an author. Poetry. Novels. She believes words can outlive us. Between them, I learned balance. Order and, imagination."

I didn't add the rest, but it sat in my heart: and my grandfather, 92, once the General Manager of Hindustan Motors, now my cricket guru and partner in laughter.

Ranjit's eyes narrowed. "But you're half this, half that. Don't you feel... rootless?"

I looked him in the eye. "No, Uncle. I feel... rooted twice in the Marina and the Ganga, in Carnatic notes and Banaarasi shaayari, in kabaddi grounds and poetry recitals. If anything, I feel I have more rivers to draw from, not less."

Silence stretched. The mist swirled.

Neena tilted her head. "And caste?"

I smiled faintly. "Since childhood, every form I filled said the same: caste—N/A. Not applicable. My parents taught me being a good human is enough. I believe the caste system should not exist. It divides what was meant to be one whole."

Ranjit's face gave nothing away, but Neena's eyes softened.

Finally, Ranjit asked, "And Aneri? What do you see in her?"

My heart thudded, but I answered honestly.

"I see someone who isn't afraid to play her own strings. I see a leader, a musician, someone who can laugh at me when I trip, but sing with me when I stand tall. I don't see a political connection or a name. I see... her."

There. Bare and unfiltered.

Ranjit studied me for a long time. Then, surprisingly, he smiled a faint, reluctant smile, but real.

"You are... unusual, Viraaj."

Neena added softly, "Unusual may be what this world needs."

They walked on, leaving me stunned in the mist.

From behind a pillar, Aneri exhaled.

She hadn't meant to eavesdrop, but her uncle's questions had pulled her in. And hearing Viraaj answer with such honesty, such clarity, without trying to impress.

She smiled. A real smile.

For the first time, she thought: maybe her family wasn't as closed as she feared. Maybe some doors could be opened.

And maybe, Viraaj had already begun unlocking them.

The Younger Dhars' Reflection

Their cottage at the resort was quieter than the rest.

Most rooms still hummed with chatter — cousins laughing, elders arguing about rituals, dhols thumping in distant corners. But in the room where Ranjit Dhar and Neena Mukhim sat, only the slow tick-tock of a clock could be heard.

Ranjit poured tea into steel tumblers. Neena took hers, though her eyes stayed fixed on the misted window.

"You're thinking of him," she said quietly.

Ranjit didn't answer at once. He sipped, then, nodded. "Yes."

"He's reckless," Ranjit muttered. "He is sharp-tongued. He mocked politics on stage, Neena. Right in front of Bah Ba."

"Yet Bah Ba didn't scold him," Neena replied.

Ranjit's lips twitched. "Not openly."

Neena turned. "And privately? Did you see his eyes? Bah Ba was... listening."

Ranjit set his tumbler down with a sigh. "Listening is not agreeing."

"But it's more than ignoring," Neena pressed. "Tell me, when was the last time you saw Bah Ba pause for a youth's words?"

Ranjit said nothing.

Neena leaned back, her voice softer now. "That boy... Viraaj. He doesn't speak like a climber, Ranjit. Not like Rishav, with his rehearsed smiles and trophy words. Viraaj speaks like someone who has been told all his life he doesn't belong, yet refuses to stop speaking anyway."

Ranjit's brow furrowed. "And you think that's strength?"

"I think that's survival," Neena said simply. "And survival makes stronger leaders than privilege ever will."

Ranjit rubbed his forehead. "Still... Bah Ba has already chosen Rishav. The families have spoken. The path is drawn. If Aneri resists too hard—"

"She will suffer," Neena finished for him. Her eyes softened with worry. "Yes. That's what frightens me."

He looked at her. "And yet... if she resists with someone like Viraaj at her side... would that frighten you less?"

Neena didn't answer right away. She thought of Viraaj's words in the garden. *"I don't see a political connection or a name. I see... her."*

Her lips curved faintly. "Perhaps, less."

Ranjit leaned back, staring at the lantern glow. "I am not saying I trust him. Not yet. But..."

"But you don't dismiss him either," Neena finished.

He nodded reluctantly.

They sat in silence, tea cooling between them. Outside, the mist wrapped the hills, as though shielding secrets.

Finally, Neena whispered, "Perhaps we should watch. Not interfere. Just... watch. Sometimes, truths reveal themselves without us forcing them."

Ranjit sighed, but his eyes softened. "Yes. We will watch."

And for the first time that week, the air in their cottage didn't feel heavy with inevitability. It felt... open.

Meanwhile, Aneri, passing by the cottage on her way to fetch her guitar, heard the faint echo of their words. She didn't linger—didn't dare. But even that brief glimpse filled her chest with something she hadn't allowed herself in days.

Hope.

Aneri's Quiet Resolve

I hadn't meant to stop outside their cottage.

I was only on my way back to fetch my guitar, my fingers itching to play out the restlessness swirling in me. But the voices — my uncle Ranjit's, my aunt Neena's — slipped through the half-open window like threads of light.

I froze. And then I listened.

"That boy... he doesn't speak like a climber. He speaks like someone who has been told all his life he doesn't belong, yet refuses to stop speaking anyway."

Aunt Neena's words.

And my uncle's silence was heavier than any sentence.

I bit my lip hard. No one in my family spoke of Viraaj like that. They dismissed him as a comedian, a journalist, a joke.

But here, for the first time, someone acknowledged the truth I'd seen since the train.

That Viraaj wasn't half-anything. He was more.

I leaned against the cool wall, heart hammering.

All week, I had felt trapped pulled like a pawn between my father's ambitions and Rishav's smug presence. I had smiled when I wanted to scream, nodded when I wanted to walk away.

But tonight, something shifted.

If my uncle who was loyal, cautious, always Bah's shadow could pause long enough to see Viraaj's worth, then maybe... maybe the walls weren't as impenetrable as I thought.

Maybe cracks existed. And through cracks, light could enter.

Viraaj in My Eyes

I closed my eyes and saw him again chutney-smeared at the festival, scooter-wiring mid-chase, clutching the milk bottle like it was a weapon. Saw him holding his ground in front of my father, words steady as rain, unafraid to debate a man who could crush him with one command.

And then I heard his voice on the stage, turning laughter into protest and, protest into hope.

How could anyone call him half?

He was whole. Entire. Overflowing.

And, me?

I wasn't sure if I was strong enough. But I knew one thing: if strength could be borrowed, if courage could be shared, then I wanted his to be mine.

The mist clung to my skin, damp and cold, but inside me, something burned.

I couldn't wait for my father's approval. I couldn't wait for Rishav to vanish. I couldn't wait for destiny to move pieces on my behalf.

If I wanted something — if I wanted Viraaj — I would have to choose quietly, secretly, stubbornly.

I placed my hand on the guitar case, the wood warm against my palm.

Yes. Music would be my rebellion. My voice, my strings, his raga — together, we would carve out a truth no one could ignore.

I whispered it to the mist, a promise no one else would hear.

"I won't let them write my song for me."

And somewhere inside, I knew: tomorrow, the resistance would begin.

Viraaj's Doubt

I had been praised, teased, even lightly scolded after the after-party, but none of it settled in my heart.

What settled was the silence of Aneri's father.
What settled were the whispers of her relatives.
What settled was the gnawing question: *Did I go too far?*

I stood alone on the balcony that night, looking over the glowing resort lawns. Laughter drifted up from the cousins' rooms. Lanterns swayed. Mist curled like questions I couldn't answer.

I replayed my words on stage, my debate with Mr. Dhar, the glint in Ranjit Uncle's eyes. Brave? Or, foolish?

Was I building bridges... or burning them?

A voice interrupted my spiral.

"Stop looking like you're in a tragic art film."

I turned. Riya — my cousin, the bride stood there, bangles clinking, her hair half undone after another round of haldi rehearsals.

"Riya," I muttered. "Don't you have a wedding to worry about?"

She smirked. "Don't *you* have a wedding to crash?"

I choked. "What?"

"Oh, don't play dumb, Viraaj," she said, leaning on the railing. "You think no one has noticed? The way you look at her? The way she looks at you? Half the cousins are already betting on when you'll trip over your own tongue and confess."

I groaned. "Riya..."

She softened. "Listen. I've heard the whispers. They don't see you as an option. But you know what? Options are boring. You're not boring. You are necessary."

I frowned. "Necessary?"

"Yes," she said firmly. "This wedding has enough politics and deals. You remind us what weddings should be—fun, laughter and honesty. What about that speech tonight? You think you made enemies? Maybe. But you also made believers. Even Bah paused. That's not small."

Her words hit deeper than I expected.

She nudged me. "Don't doubt yourself. If you're scared, it means you care. And if you care, you're already halfway there."

I laughed softly. "When did you get so wise?"

"Bridal hormones," she deadpanned.

For the first time that night, the knot in my chest loosened.

The Groom Speaks

The next afternoon, while aunties argued over whether the baaraat should start with drums or conches, I found myself dragged to the groom's suite.

"Aneri's cousin wants to see you," a younger cousin whispered with a grin.

Inside, the groom, Arvind Mukhim sat cross-legged on the bed, still in half-wedding clothes, nerves clear in his twitching hands.

He waved me in. "Viraaj bhaiya. Sit."

For a while, silence hung. Then he sighed.

"I don't know why I called you. Maybe because you say things no one else says."

I waited.

He fiddled with his cuff. "They're pushing Aneri too badly. Rishav, his family, *a Kha*... it's all pressure. She smiles, but I know her. She's not happy. And I can't do anything. I'm the groom, Viraaj.

I'm supposed to focus on my own wedding, not my cousin's life. But..." His voice cracked. "I hate watching it."

I swallowed.

He looked up, eyes tired. "You stood up on the stage, in front of everyone. You said what no one dares. I admired that. And I think she admires it too."

"Arvind—" I began.

He raised a hand. "Don't say anything. Just... if you care for her, don't back down. Please. Someone has to fight for her. If not her family, then, maybe you."

He extended his hand. For a second, I hesitated — then gripped it.

It wasn't a grand alliance. Not a dramatic promise. But it was something.

A cousin's quiet blessing.

And as I left his room, I realized: Aneri wasn't as alone as she thought. Neither was I.

The Groom's Reflection

After Viraaj left the room, the air felt heavier.

Arvind Mukhim sat back on the bed, staring at his own reflection in the mirror. The mirror didn't lie: his collar sat awkward; his shoulders slumped. He looked less like a groom, more like a boy trapped in clothes too heavy for him.

He pressed his palms together, leaning forward.

It wasn't fair. This was supposed to be *his* week. His wedding to Riya Raghuvanshi, a girl he'd grown to love after years of awkward interactions and family-approved meetings. It was a good match and, a happy one.

But instead of focusing on vows, on rituals, on the smile that Riya carried like sunshine, his mind churned with shadows. Aneri's shadows.

His sister-cousin, his childhood playmate pulled like a puppet by Laishon *a Kha* — his older uncle, the father-figure whose word had always been law.

Rishav's arrival had tilted everything- the power, the politics, and the suffocating expectation that Aneri would smile and comply to.

And, Arvind? He had done nothing. Could do nothing.

"I should protect her," he whispered to the empty room.

But, how? He was the groom, the centre piece of ceremonies. Every eye would be on him. Every word, every laugh would be measured. If he rebelled now, he would risk not just his wedding, but Riya's joy too.

Yet, every time he saw Aneri's forced smiles, he felt like a coward.

Then came Viraaj- The clumsy, milk-drinking, chutney-stained Viraaj who had somehow, without permission, stepped where no one else dared. Who mocked politics on stage. Who debated Laishon *a Kha* without fear. Who made people laugh — but also made them think.

Arvind envied him. But more than envy, he admired him.

He remembered the handshake — Viraaj's grip steady, his eyes unflinching. For a moment, Arvind had felt something he hadn't in days.

Hope.

Arvind rubbed his forehead. "I can't fight. Not openly. But... I can believe in him. Maybe that's something."

He thought of Riya, of her laughter, of the future he wanted with her. Then, he thought of Aneri, of the chains tightening around her.

"I'll keep silent," he muttered. "But silence doesn't mean I don't care."

He didn't know if Viraaj had the strength to fight. He didn't know if Aneri would resist.

But he knew this: if anyone could change the script, it wasn't him.

It was Viraaj.

The Sister's Secret

Riya's kept tracing the designs of the henna on her palms as though memorizing them forever. She sat by her window, the moonlight catching her bangles, her face glowing with the half-exhaustion, half-euphoria of a bride.

That's where Aneri found her.

"Still awake?" Aneri whispered, slipping inside.

Riya looked up, her smile quick and mischievous. "Still brooding?"

Aneri sat cross-legged on the bed. For a while, neither spoke. The silence between women in a family that busy was rare, precious.

Finally, Aneri said it. "Riya... can I tell you something? Something I can't tell anyone else?"

Riya's eyes sparkled. "If it's about Viraaj, I already know."

Aneri choked. "What—"

Riya laughed softly. “The way you two look at each other? Please. Half the cousins are already placing bets.”

Aneri groaned, hiding her face. “Why is everyone betting on us?”

“Because,” Riya said gently, “they can see what you are trying to hide. But go on. Say it anyway.”

Aneri stared at her hands, twisting her bangles.

“They’re pushing me harder every day. Rishav this, Rishav that. It’s suffocating. And I’ve been… smiling through it. Pretending.”

Her voice dropped. “But I don’t want to be with him. Not even a little. And I can’t keep pretending anymore.”

Riya listened, her face calm, her eyes steady.

“I don’t know if I am brave enough to fight loudly,” Aneri admitted. “But I can resist. Quietly, in my own way with music, with truth, with… him.”

The last word hung heavy between them.

For a moment, Riya said nothing. Then she leaned forward, her hand covering Aneri’s.

“You think you’re not brave, Aneri. But do you know how much courage it takes to even whisper ‘no?’ To even dream of something else when everyone around you has already written your script?”

Aneri’s throat tightened.

Riya's smile softened. "You don't need to be loud. You just need to be you. And if music is your rebellion, then let it be the loudest silence they've ever heard."

Aneri blinked, tears pricking. "So, you'll stand with me?"

"Of course," Riya said simply. "You'll be my sister soon. Sisters don't let each other fight alone."

They sat there in the dim light, two women on opposite ends of fate — one already stepping into marriage, one resisting being forced into it.

Aneri's resolve, once a private whisper to herself, now had a witness. A sister.

And in that quiet room, without drums or rituals, a pact was born.

She would resist.
Riya would stand with her.
And maybe, together, they could change the ending.

Sisters in the Night

The room was hushed, the air heavy with the faint scent of henna and sandalwood.

Riya leaned back against the headboard, her bridal bangles clinking as she toyed with her dupatta. Aneri sat cross-legged at the foot of the bed, her guitar propped beside her.

The silence between them was thick, but not uncomfortable.

"Can I tell you something, Aneri?" Riya said suddenly, her voice softer than usual.

Aneri blinked. "Of course."

Riya stared at her henna-stained hands. "I'm terrified."

Aneri frowned. "Terrified? But you and Arvind..."

"Yes, yes, I know. We love each other. We agreed to this. Everyone thinks I'm the happiest bride alive. And I am. But... marriage isn't just about two people. It's about families. Expectation, roles, sacrifices."

Her voice trembled slightly. “What if I can’t live up to it all? What if I lose myself in the process?”

Aneri’s chest tightened. “Riya...”

“I watch you,” Riya said, eyes glistening. “You’re fighting quietly. And part of me envies that. But that doesn’t mean I’m not afraid.”

Aneri shook her head. “But you’re brave in your own way. You chose him. That’s more than many brides can say. And Arvind looks at you like you are the only person in the room. That’s something.”

Riya smiled faintly. “You noticed?”

“Of course,” Aneri said softly. “Love shows.”

Riya leaned forward; eyes steady now. “Then listen to me, Aneri. If your heart doesn’t want Rishav, don’t let anyone force you. Not your father, not the whispers of relatives. Because living a life you never chose is worse than facing their anger.”

Aneri swallowed hard, her throat aching. “But what if I disappoint everyone?”

“You will,” Riya said bluntly. “at least, once in your life. So why not disappoint them by being true to yourself?”

The words hit like thunder wrapped in tenderness.

For a long time, they sat in silence, both processing their fears, their hopes, their unspoken prayers.

Then Riya reached out, grabbing Aneri's hand. "Whatever happens, you're not alone. I'll be your sister, in name and in heart. And if you need me—at the mandap (wedding stage), in the chaos, anywhere—I'll stand beside you."

Aneri's eyes burned. She nodded, gripping Riya's hand back.

And in that quiet, moonlit room, the pact between them deepened.

Songs between Sisters

The clock ticked closer to midnight, but neither Aneri nor Riya were ready to sleep.

The air smelled faintly of roses and turmeric, leftovers from the rituals. The faint hum of a dhol (instrument like a drum played with sticks) drifted in from another wing of the resort, where younger cousins were still too wired to rest.

In their quiet room, though, there was only soft laughter and the low strum of strings.

Aneri adjusted the tuning pegs on her acoustic guitar, the familiar comfort grounding her. She glanced at Riya, who was inspecting the deep brown stains of her mehendi.

“You don’t regret it?” Aneri teased.

Riya wrinkled her nose. “Not the art. It’s dried now, thankfully. I can’t imagine you ever sitting still for this.”

“You are right,” Aneri said with a laugh. “I am not so fond of mehendi. Viraaj too, actually.”

They shared a grin at that, a secret knowledge binding them further.

"So, what should we sing?" Aneri asked, strumming softly.

Riya thought for a moment, then, her voice softened. "Something... free. Something that feels like letting go."

Aneri tilted her head, then began the opening chords of a song she loved — a haunting, tender ballad, "Qayde Se – Reprise" by Shilpa Rao from *Metro... In Dino*.

Riya's eyes widened. "Perfect."

The first notes floated into the misty night, Aneri's voice clear, deep with years of practice, tinged with her songwriter's soul. Riya joined a beat later, her tone softer, not polished like Aneri's, but honest.

Two voices, one practiced, one raw, weaving into each other.

The song spoke of cages — rules, boundaries, chains — and the yearning to break them, to breathe free.

And in that moment, it wasn't just a song. It was confession. Resistance. Hope.

Aneri watched Riya as she sang, her hands lifting instinctively with her face glowing with something more than bridal excitement.

"You are good," Aneri whispered when they paused.

Riya smiled. "Maybe not good. But honest."

"That's all music needs to be," Aneri said.

They played on, voices mingling; laughter spilling when one missed a note, only to find the harmony again.

By the time the last chord faded, the sisters sat in silence, hearts thudding, eyes bright.

"We'll be sisters soon," Riya whispered, her voice thick. "Not just by this marriage. By choice. By song."

Aneri gripped her hand. "By song," she repeated.

Neither said it aloud, but both felt it: this wouldn't be the last time they sang together.

In the years ahead, through fights and reconciliations, through family storms and celebrations, this night would remain their first duet.

The song sang not of cages, but of freedom.

The guitar rested silent now, but the song lingered between them like perfume. Aneri and Riya sat cross-legged on the bed, their laughter finally fading into a comfortable hush.

For a while, they simply listened to the sounds outside — muffled dhols, faint cousin chatter, and the occasional burst of fireworks.

Then Riya broke the silence.

"Aneri," she said softly, "can I tell you something I haven't told anyone? Not even Arvind?"

Aneri leaned closer. "Of course."

Riya fiddled with the edge of her dupatta; her eyes thoughtful. "Everyone keeps asking me about jewellery, clothes, and rituals. But what I think about most isn't the wedding day. It's... after."

Aneri tilted her head. "After?"

Riya nodded, a shy smile playing on her lips. "Like... I want to set up a tiny balcony garden. Just tulsi, marigold, maybe some tomatoes. Nothing fancy, just a garden that's mine."

Aneri blinked — surprised by the simplicity, then smiled.

"And," Riya continued, giggling, "I want a dog. A ridiculously, fluffy one. Arvind doesn't even know I've already picked a name. *Golu.*"

They both burst out laughing at the image of a fat dog waddling through a new home.

"But it's not just that," Riya said, her smile softening. "I dream of dinners where Arvind and I argue about who cooks better daal (lentil), of teaching my kids to dance before they learn to walk. Of going to Banaras someday with him and eating litti chokha (wheat balls stuffed with roasted gram flour served with roasted vegetable mash) on the Ghats."

She sighed. "But that's what makes life worth it, na? Not the politics. Not the show but the small, ordinary joys. Right?"

Aneri swallowed hard, her throat thick. "And what if it doesn't happen that way?"

Riya looked straight at her. "Then I'll fight for it quietly, loudly. Whatever it takes."

Aneri's eyes burned. "Aren't you scared?"

"Of course, I'm scared," Riya admitted. "Everyone is. But fear doesn't mean surrender. Fear means you care about what's at stake."

She reached for Aneri's hand, squeezing it tight. "So don't run from your fear, Aneri. Use it. Let it tell you what matters most."

Aneri couldn't speak. She only nodded, her chest aching with both love and determination.

Riya smiled, her bridal bangles catching the moonlight. "Someday, when you're a bride, I'll sit on your bed and remind you of this night. And we'll laugh about how we sang songs instead of sleeping."

Aneri laughed through the lump in her throat. "And about your fat dog, Golu."

They both dissolved into giggles, and in that laughter, fear didn't vanish — but it felt smaller. Bearable.

Interrupted, but Not Broken

The room still hummed with the echoes of their laughter when the door burst open.

Three younger cousins tumbled inside, all of them giggling, their eyes wide with mischief.

"Didi!" one squealed. "Why are you awake so late? Singing songs instead of sleeping? The bride will get dark circles!"

Riya rolled her eyes but smiled. "Better dark circles than dark in-laws," she shot back, making Aneri choke on her laughter.

Another cousin, barely sixteen, pointed dramatically at Aneri's guitar. "Are you two forming a secret band? Shall we name it *Shaadi Sisters*?"

Riya smirked. "Only if you are our backup dancers."

The cousins collapsed in giggles, draping themselves across the bed like they owned it. One even tried strumming the guitar, plucking painfully wrong notes until Aneri rescued it with mock indignation.

The cousins demanded a song, a funny one. Aneri and Riya exchanged a look, a silent agreement.

They strummed a silly tune together, improvising ridiculous lyrics about aunties fighting over mehendi designs and uncles dozing mid-dhol. The room shook with laughter, the younger cousins howling until they fell over each other.

To anyone outside, it was just harmless fun. Two girls teasing each other before sleep.

But beneath the laughter, Aneri felt the weight of their earlier pact still humming like a secret chord.

As the cousins finally tired and sprawled across the floor with blankets, Riya caught Aneri's eye.

She raised her mehendi-stained hand and tapped her wrist twice — their newly invented signal. It meant: *I'm here. We're in this together.*

Aneri tapped the guitar's wood twice in return. *I know.*

Her heart raced, not with fear, but with something new. Thrill.

For the first time, she felt what it was like to carry a rebellion not alone, but with someone else holding half the weight.

It was dangerous. It was risky.

But it was also exhilarating.

And as she finally lay down, guitar resting beside her, Aneri smiled into the darkness.

Tomorrow, the song would change.

Parallel Strength

The resort was buzzing that morning.

Cousins darted through the halls with trays of sweets. Aunties fought over saari pleats. Rishav strutted around like he owned the place, rehearsing his smile for invisible cameras.

And me? I slipped out to the quiet side of the garden; phone in hand, heart heavier than the drums pounding in the courtyard.

I dialled home.

"Viraaj?" Pa's voice was crisp, measured, like the ticking of a railway clock. Even through the phone, I could picture him in his starched white shirt, spectacles sliding down his nose.

"Pa," I said softly. "I... needed to hear your voice."

He paused, then said, "What's troubling you, son?"

I hesitated. "I feel like I'm... running in circles. I speak, they dismiss me. I act, they laugh. I want to be accepted, Pa, but it feels like shouting into a storm."

There was a pause. Then his voice, calm and sharp:

“Do you remember the shruti box?”

“Yes,” I whispered.

“Hours of the same note. Again and again, until your throat ached.”

I smiled faintly. “Yes.”

“That note wasn’t about perfection. It was about patience. Discipline. To hold steady when everything shakes. Viraaj, the world won’t adjust in a day. But if you keep striking your note, one day, they’ll hear it. That is your discipline. That is your strength.”

His words settled deep, steadying my chest like ballast on a train.

And then I heard her.

“Beta?” Mumma’s voice, warm as poetry, soft as Banaras Ghats at dusk.

“Mumma,” I breathed.

“You sound tired,” she said immediately.

“I’m fine,” I lied.

“No,” she said, gently scolding. “Your voice is restless. Speak.”

I sighed. “I want to be seen, Mumma. I want to be more than just a half this, half that. But... sometimes it feels like no matter what I do, I’ll never belong fully anywhere.”

Her silence was long, patient. Then she said:

"Viraaj, you've always wanted to belong everywhere. But the truth is, you don't need everyone. You just need the ones who see you truly. Do not waste your courage chasing shadows. Use it to light the people standing beside you."

I closed my eyes.

"Words, beta," she continued. "They can't always win battles. But they can win hearts. Speak your heart, write your truth, and sing your note even if it cracks. That's where courage lives."

I swallowed hard; throat thick. "Pa... Mumma... thank you."

"Remember," Pa said firmly, "a railway engine doesn't stop every time the crowd boos. It runs its course. You must too."

"And remember," Mumma added softly, "a poem doesn't ask for applause. It just wants to be true."

Their words filled me, one like iron, and the other like water. Discipline and poetry. Roots and wings.

I exhaled, lighter than I had felt in days.

"Pa, Mumma," I whispered. "I'll try."

"No," Mumma corrected gently. "You'll do."

Pa spoke again. "Viraj, can I tell you something more if you have a few more minutes?"

"Yes, Pa?"

"Years ago," Pa said, "Before you were born, I was just a young man working in Southern Railway. I was enthusiastic about my first official railway program."

I closed my eyes, letting his words paint the picture.

"All the senior officials were there. It was a big event. I was nervous, of course. And then, one of the highest-ranking officers asked me — no, ordered me — to carry his briefcase in front of everyone."

Pa's voice dipped, quiet but unyielding. "Viraaj, in that moment, it felt like the world stopped. If I refused, I would look arrogant. If I agreed, I would betray my own dignity. Everyone's eyes were on me. My peers whispered: 'Just carry it. Don't create a scene.' Even my seniors looked at me as if to say: bend. This is how things work."

He paused. "But I stood my ground."

"I said clearly: 'Sir, my job does not require me to carry anyone's briefcase. I am here to do my duty, and I will do it with respect. But not this.'"

My heart thudded in my chest, as though I was standing there beside him.

"For a second, Viraaj, it felt like I had lost everything. That moment of silence was heavy. I thought I would be punished. Transferred. Forgotten."

"And then?" I whispered.

“And then,” Pa said, his voice lifting with memory, “I earned their respect. Not immediately, but slowly. My juniors, my peers, even the seniors. They saw I would not bend for power. They knew they could trust me to be honest, to be fair. And now at so much higher a post, I still carry that truth. That courage. It has never failed me.”

He let the silence settle. Then, he continued, “Viraaj, you don’t need to shout to be brave. Sometimes, courage is simply saying ‘no’ when everyone expects you to bow. Do your job. Live your truth. Don’t bend because the world demands it. If your cause is just, people will see it. Maybe not today. But someday.”

I swallowed hard; throat thick.

Pa’s words weren’t just advice. They were a mirror. His moment on that railway platform was my moment now, in this wedding storm.

“Pa,” I whispered, “thank you.”

His tone softened. “Remember, son. Don’t carry anyone’s luggage emotional or otherwise. Not in railways. Not in politics. Not in life.”

I wasn’t just his son. I was his legacy.

And tomorrow, I would carry that courage into my own storm.

Before I had time to reflect more, Mumma’s voice floated through the line, warm and melodic. “Beta, so, Pa told you one of his railway stories?”

I laughed softly. "Yes, about the briefcase."

She chuckled knowingly. "He loves that one. Always did. But I have my own story for you tonight. Will you listen?"

"As always," I replied.

"When I was a girl," she began, "I wanted to write. Not for fame. Not for money. Just... because it felt like breathing. Words made sense of the world when nothing else did. For me, writing was the best job in the world, even if no one else thought so."

Her tone softened. "But your Naanu (maternal grandfather) thought it was foolish. He'd say, 'Writers and poets are only remembered when they are dead. What use is it now?' He wanted me to find a serious job. Stable. A respectable one."

I felt my chest tighten. "And you?"

"I didn't give up," she said simply.

"I kept writing small poems, short stories. I kept sending them to magazines and newspapers. One day, one of my poems was published in a magazine for youngsters. And with it came a letter, asking me to contribute more accompanied with a cheque. My first pay check."

Her laugh was soft, nostalgic. "When I showed it to Naana, he was... shocked. He didn't say much. No praise. No permission. But I saw it in his eyes he was pleased."

I pictured my 92-year-old grandfather, cricket-mad and stubborn, younger then, frowning at a daughter who refused to bend.

"And still," Mumma continued, "he wouldn't say he approved. So, I kept going. I wrote and got published more. I earned little but enough. Until finally, one day, I became a radio jockey at All India Radio in Chennai. My voice carried across the city. People knew me and appreciated me."

Her tone swelled with quiet pride. "Then, I became a cultural correspondent at Plus Channel. And do you know what happened? Slowly, Naana began to admire me. He even started his own scriptwriting, inspired by me. The man who once mocked writing as useless picked up the pen himself."

Her voice steadied; warm and fierce all at once.

"Beta, truth outlives walls. Words outlive silence. If I had bent, if I had listened to everyone who said 'no,' I would not be the woman I am. I did not wait for approval. I did not surrender. I wrote again and again until the world had no choice but to read."

I sat very still; my throat thick.

"Mumma..." I whispered.

"You are my son," she said firmly. "You carry my pen and your Pa's discipline. You are double. You are whole. You are truth in motion."

Tears stung my eyes.

Pa had taught me to stand tall, to refuse to carry a luggage which wasn't mine.
Mumma had taught me to keep writing, keep speaking, even when no one listened.

Together, their voices braided inside me — discipline and poetry, steel and silk.

And I realized: I didn't just come from rivers and seas. I came from battles already fought, already won.

Now it was my turn.

As the call ended, I looked up at the hills. The mist was lifting.

I didn't know what the day would bring. But I knew this: I wasn't half. I wasn't less.

I was double, twice-rooted. And ready.

Ink in the Mist

The morning mist hung low, curling around the resort like a shawl.

Most of the household was still asleep after last night's chaos, but I sat outside on the veranda with my old leather journal — the one Mumma had given me when I first went to college.

The cover was scratched, the pages crinkled, but it still felt like home.

Her voice echoed in me from last night's call.

"Truth outlives walls. Words outlive silence. If I had bent, I would not be the woman I am today."

I touched pen to paper, hesitant at first. My handwriting, always a mix of Tamil and Hindi quirks, wobbled across the page.

> *Pa says never carry anyone's baggage.*
> *Mumma says never stop writing, even when no one listens.*
> *Maybe my job is to carry my own words. Always. No matter how heavy.*

I paused, tapping the pen.

> *The world doesn't need another politician. The world doesn't need another businessman. The world needs voices — stubborn, foolish, insistent voices that won't stop singing even when drowned out.*

My hand steadied as I wrote.

> *I will not shout to be heard. I will not beg to belong. I will speak. Write. Laugh. Sing.*
>
> *Word by word, joke by joke, raga by raga — until even walls shall listen.*
>
> *My words will outlive me. My truths will outlast fear. That is my vow.*

I stopped, staring at the ink.

For the first time in days, the storm inside me felt quieter. Not gone, but shaped.

As I closed the journal, I remembered something odd.

Laishon Dhar, Aneri's father had quoted lines during dinner once, lines about youth, politics, and generational weakness; lines that had sounded strangely familiar.

I hadn't thought much of it then. But now, with Mumma's story fresh, I wondered...

No. It was probably coincidence.

Still, the echo of those words lingered, like a door half-open, waiting for me to push through.

I tucked the journal under my arm, feeling lighter.

Today would bring its own chaos — Rishav's rehearsals, aunties' gossip, the endless swirl of rituals. But in my pocket now was something stronger than fear.

It was a vow in ink. It was a promise to myself.

And I knew when the time came; those words would carry me through.

Comic Interruption

The morning rituals had wound down, leaving the courtyard alive with chaos — aunties haggling over flower arrangements, uncles arguing about seating, Rishav smirking like a Bollywood villain in rehearsal.

I slipped quietly toward the garden, my eyes catching Aneri's across the crowd. She tilted her head just slightly, guitar case in hand.

A signal.

But, before we could disappear, three cousins appeared out of nowhere like comic-book sidekicks.

"Arrey, Viraaj bhaiya!" one shouted. "Where are you sneaking off to? Going to practice your comedy amidst the trees?"

Aneri rolled her eyes. "Grow up, you monkeys."

But they weren't letting go. One even mimed holding a guitar dramatically. "Love duet practice?"

The heat rose to my ears. “No! We were just... going to fix the sound system.”

“Sound system?” a cousin cackled. “With a guitar?”

Quick on her feet, Aneri added dryly, “Yes, obviously. Guitars are the new screwdrivers.”

The cousins howled with laughter, then finally ran off, promising to “report to the elders” if we disappeared too long.

Aneri groaned. “We’ll need better cover stories.”

I grinned. “Or better cousins.”

Later that afternoon, I found myself cornered by the cousins again — but this time, willingly.

They dragged me to the veranda with chai cups and demanded, “Do some stand-up, bhaiya! Just five minutes! We need entertainment before tonight’s chaos.”

I hesitated. Then I remembered my vow in ink that morning. *My words will outlive walls.*

Maybe this was practice.

So, I stood, cleared my throat, and began.

“Indian weddings are like railway stations. Everyone arrives late, nobody knows the schedule, and somehow, there are always ten extra passengers no one invited.”

Laughter erupted. Encouraged, I pushed further.

"And politicians? They're like wedding photographers. Always in the frame, never part of the family, and charging way too much for blurry results!"

The cousins doubled over. Even a nearby auntie chuckled before pretending she hadn't heard.

I finished softer. "But you know what weddings teach us? That even chaos has rhythm. Even strangers can become family. And sometimes, the best parts are the unplanned — like a cousin tripping on stage, or a joke landing better than expected."

Applause rung in the air which felt genuine and affectionate.

And in that moment, I felt it — the truth of Mumma's words. Laughter could be courage too.

Silent Resistance

Evening crept over the hills, painting the resort gold. The courtyard buzzed with rehearsals — cousins from Rishav's side practicing stiff moves, aunties clapping along half-heartedly.

But Aneri wasn't there.

She slipped away quietly, guitar on her back, pulling me with her.

We found a quiet terrace overlooking the misty valley, lanterns swaying gently.

She set the guitar down "Ready?"

I raised an eyebrow. "For what?"

"For resistance," she said simply.

She strummed a soft chord, her voice low and steady. I followed with a Carnatic raga, weaving into her melody.

At first, it was clumsy — her strings pulling one way, my notes another. But slowly, it clicked. Her guitar became the river, my raga the current. Together, they flowed.

The song wasn't for the wedding. It wasn't for the families. It was for us; a secret confession in melody, louder than any spoken word.

She looked at me as she sang, her eyes sparking with defiance and something gentler, warmer.

For a heartbeat, the world shrank — no Rishav, no rituals, and no politics. Just two people finding freedom in music.

When the final note faded, the silence was thunderous.

She whispered, breathless, "This is ours. Our resistance."

I nodded, heart hammering. "Our truth."

Neither of us noticed the shadow of a cousin slipping away, eyes wide, having overheard.

Tomorrow, secrets would begin to crack.

But tonight, we had our song.

Love as Resistance

The terrace had gone silent after our song, the hills swallowing the last echo of her guitar. Aneri and I lingered in that silence, hearts racing, before slipping back separately into the chaos of the resort.

But I couldn't sleep that night.

I sat at my desk in the dim light of a single lamp, my journal open. The ink from Mumma's lesson still fresh on the previous page.

I stared at the blank sheet. Then, slowly, I wrote.

> *Today, we sang. Not for applause. Not for anyone else but for ourselves. Her strings, my voice — they didn't ask for permission, and they didn't bend for approval. They just were.*

I paused, remembering her eyes as she sang — fire and softness, rebellion and confession.

> *Maybe love isn't flowers and fireworks. Maybe love is resistance. Standing still when the world demands you move, singing when silence is safer, looking at*

> *someone and saying, "I see you," when everyone else ignores you.*

My pen scratched faster.

> *Pa taught me not to carry someone else's baggage... Mumma taught me not to stop writing, even when no one reads. And tonight, Aneri taught me: love can be the loudest 'no' and the quietest 'yes' at the same time.*

I leaned back, exhaling.

This wasn't just about romance anymore. This was about choosing truth, even if it cost everything.

And I realized something that made my chest tighten with both fear and hope:

If standing with her meant standing against the world, I would.

I closed the journal, whispering softly into the empty room:

"Our song will outlive their walls."

And for the first time, the weight of the storm ahead didn't feel unbearable.

It felt necessary.

The Eavesdropper

The cousin who had witnessed our song on the terrace hadn't meant to overhear. Not really.

He had just wandered up to the terrace looking for extra sweets hidden away from greedy hands. But instead of laddoos (a popular Indian sweet made from a mixture of various kinds of flour, sugar and ghee which is shaped into a ball), he'd found something far juicier: Aneri strumming her guitar, Viraaj singing beside her, voices twined like secret threads in the mist.

He froze, wide eyed, listening just long enough to understand.

Then he slipped away.

By morning, the whispers floated through the resort like smoke.

"They were together last night."
"On the terrace singing alone."
"Did you hear the way he looked at her?"

Most cousins dismissed it with teasing. But a few aunties caught scent of scandal, their voices sharp.

"Not proper."
"Not dignified."
"She's being courted by Rishav!"

The whispers never reached Laishon Dhar directly — not yet. But they slithered close enough to brush against ears that mattered.

And Aneri felt it, in the sidelong glances, in the laughter that lingered too long, in the sudden hush whenever she walked into a room.

"Viraaj," she whispered when they finally met in the corridor. "People are gossiping."

His jaw tightened. "About the song?"

"Yes."

He exhaled, slow. "Let them whisper."

"But—"

He caught her gaze, his eyes calm. "Let them whisper. We sang for us. If truth makes them uneasy, maybe it's because they have forgotten what truth sounds like."

Her heart ached at his steadiness. But the knot in her stomach remained.

Whispers could become storms. And storms always found roofs to break.

Rishav's Frustration

The storm broke sooner than expected.

It was during the rehearsal for the groom's baaraat, in the middle of the courtyard. Drums thundered, uncles clapped, cousins danced in mock formation. Aneri was supposed to stand beside Rishav, smiling as he gestured grandly, playing the part of the perfect pair.

But she didn't.

Her smile faltered. Her eyes kept darting toward the side lines, where Viraaj stood with the bride's cousins, laughing quietly.

Rishav noticed.

"Stand properly," he hissed at her under his breath.

Aneri stiffened. "I am."

"No, you're not," he muttered, loud enough that nearby cousins glanced over. "You're distracted. Do you think this is a joke?"

Aneri froze, her face burning.

And then, in front of everyone, Rishav's voice snapped sharp:

"Can you stop acting like a child and focus for once?"

The courtyard stilled.

The cousins exchanged uneasy glances. An aunt cleared her throat. Even the drummer faltered.

Aneri's cheeks flamed, humiliation burning in her chest. She opened her mouth, but words failed.

And from the side lines, Viraaj stepped forward half a pace — not speaking, not yet, but his presence was enough to make Rishav's jaw clench tighter.

"Don't embarrass me again," Rishav muttered before turning back to the rehearsal, his smile plastered on like cheap paint.

But the crack had shown.

And for the first time, everyone had seen it.

The rehearsal ended in scattered laughter, but the air was tight. Everyone tried to move on, but the cousins' eyes lingered too long, the aunties' whispers cut too sharp.

Aneri didn't speak then. She walked off quietly, her dupatta dragging across the courtyard tiles. But her silence wasn't surrender. It was a fuse.

And when Rishav caught up with her behind the resort's side corridor, the fuse lit.

"What was that?" she hissed, whirling on him.

Rishav frowned. "What was what?"

"You humiliated me in front of everyone."

His jaw tightened. "I told you to focus. You weren't focussing. Do you want people to think you can't even stand beside me properly?"

Her eyes blazed. "Do you hear yourself? Stand beside you properly? I'm not a prop, Rishav."

He stepped closer, lowering his voice. "Then stop acting like one. You think this is about you? This is bigger. Families. Politics. Images. If you embarrass me—"

She cut him off, her voice sharp as glass. "Embarrass you? Or show people the truth of who you are?"

For the first time, Rishav faltered. His mask slipped — just slightly — before he forced it back.

"You don't understand," he muttered. "You've been sheltered. You don't know how the world works."

Aneri's laugh was bitter. "Maybe I don't. But I know one thing: if the world requires me to be silent while someone talks down to me, then it's not a world worth standing in."

Her words hung heavy in the corridor.

Rishav leaned in, his smile cold. "Careful, Aneri. You think you're brave because you can talk back. But one day, you'll realize you've burned all your bridges. And when you do, don't expect anyone to stand with you."

Aneri's heart hammered, but she didn't flinch. She held his gaze.

"Better to burn bridges," she said, "than live my whole life on one I never chose."

She turned on her heel, leaving him in the corridor, the echo of her footsteps louder than any drumbeat.

From the shadows, Viraaj had seen enough to piece it together. He didn't step in. It wasn't his battle in that moment but his chest burned.

If she could face Rishav like that, then so could he.

And this storm, he realized, wouldn't stay private much longer.

Family Rumblings

The courtyard hummed with gossip after rehearsal, louder than the dhols.

"Poor boy, he was only asking her to focus…" one aunt sniffed.
"Poor? He snapped like a stick," another countered, shaking her head.
"He's right though. A girl should learn discipline before marriage."
"Discipline, yes. Humiliation, no."

The murmurs grew. Uncles pretended not to notice, fiddling with betel leaves. Cousins exchanged raised eyebrows, delighting in drama but wary of being caught in the middle.

And though no one spoke too loudly, the truth had already spread: Rishav's mask had cracked.

At the elders' table, the debate sharpened.

Some muttered, "He comes from power, he must keep control. That's natural."
Others whispered, "But control in public? Not a good sign."

Laishon Dhar sat in silence, his face unreadable. He neither defended his would-be son-in-law nor condemned him. That silence was louder than any verdict.

From the edge of the room, I watched.

The family wasn't one voice anymore. Cracks were showing — tiny, almost invisible, but there.

And in those cracks, maybe, light could slip in.

Later that night, while aunties fussed over jewellery and uncles debated seating charts, Riya found Aneri alone in the bridal suite.

"You," she said, closing the door behind her, "were magnificent."

Aneri blinked. "Magnificent?"

"Yes," Riya said firmly. "Do you know how many brides dream of saying what you said today? Of standing up to someone who thinks he can snap and command like a schoolmaster? You didn't just stand up — you stood tall."

Aneri flushed. "I wasn't magnificent. I was furious."

"Good," Riya grinned. "Fury is honest. And sometimes honesty is the bravest thing we can give."

But her smile faded. She sat beside Aneri, lowering her voice. "Just... be careful. Rishav doesn't like being defied. Men like him... they don't calm down when challenged. They escalate."

Aneri swallowed hard. "I know. But I can't pretend anymore."

"Then don't," Riya said softly. "Pretend nothing. But don't fight alone either. Not when you have me. Not when you have..." Her eyes flicked knowingly toward the corridor where Viraaj had been earlier.

Aneri bit her lip, warmth rising in her cheeks.

Riya took her hand. "You're not alone, Aneri. Remember that."

Aneri nodded, her chest swelling with both fear and strength.

For the first time in days, she believed it.

Midnight Journal

The night was heavy with mist again, but inside me, there was clarity.

I had watched it all — Rishav snapping like a whip, the family whispering, Aneri standing tall despite the sting. And I had seen the fear in her eyes afterward, quickly masked but not gone.

I knew then: silence was no longer an option.

I opened my journal again, the ink from Mumma's call still drying on the last page. My pen hovered. Then I wrote:

> *She burned today, but no one stood beside her. That ends now.*

I thought of Pa's story — refusing to carry someone else's baggage.
I thought of Mumma's story — refusing to stop writing even when the world mocked.
And now, Aneri's story — refusing to bow down when humiliation came like thunder.

They weren't separate stories. They were threads weaving into mine.

> *I will not let her fight alone. Not in shadows. Not in whispers. Not against a man who sees her as a prize, not a person.*

The words spilled like fire across the page.

> *If she burns, I burn beside her. If she sings, I sing with her. If she resists, I resist too. That is my truth. That is my love.*

I put the pen down, heart pounding, but strangely light.

For the first time, I understood what Pa meant about discipline, what Mumma meant about words, and what love meant when it stopped being safe.

It wasn't about being accepted.
It was about being true.

I closed the journal and whispered to the mist:

"She will never stand-alone again."

I paused, pen tapping against the page, when movement brushed the corner of my vision.

Aneri.

She was walking back to her room, her dupatta trailing, and guitar case slung over her shoulder. She slowed as she passed my window, glancing in.

Our eyes met.

She tilted her head, curious, her lips parting slightly at the sight of my open journal.

I leaned forward, pushing the window open. “Hey,” I whispered.

“Hey,” she echoed softly, stepping closer.

For a moment, neither of us spoke. Just two people framed by a window, like a scene stolen from a quiet film.

“What are you writing?” she asked.

“Just... promises,” I said.

Her brows lifted. “To whom?”

I smiled faintly. “To myself. To... us.”

Her cheeks flushed in the pale moonlight. “Do you always make everything sound like a poem?”

I chuckled. “Blame Mumma. And maybe you.”

Her smile grew softer. “Keep writing, Viraaj. Whatever happens... keep writing.”

“I will,” I whispered.

And though we didn’t touch, the space between us felt full — of unspoken trust, of fragile hope, of something stronger than both.

Later, my head heavy and I fell asleep over the journal.

And in my dream, the worlds blurred.

I stood on the Ghats of Banaras, the Ganga glowing gold under morning light. The chants of priests swirled, only to melt into the steady thrum of a mridangam (a classical double-headed South Indian drum used in Carnatic music and other traditional Indian performances) somewhere behind me.

I turned, and suddenly I was in Chennai, the Marina waves crashing, filter coffee stalls humming, Carnatic ragas floating like gulls overhead.

Then, mist rolled in, and the hills of Shillong rose before me, dotted with bamboo stalls and children flying kites that sparkled like fireflies. Aneri's laughter echoed, mingling with Mumma's poetry, Pa's discipline, and my own stumbling jokes.

All three places overlapped, rivers and seas and hills merging into one landscape.

And in the centre, I stood — not torn between anything or anyone, but tied to all.

Half of nothing.
Double of everything.

I woke with the dawn, the journal still open beneath my cheek, my vow etched both in ink and in dream.

The Mask falls again

The wedding resort buzzed louder with each passing day. Drums never seemed to stop, cousins spilled haldi onto the wrong trays, and laughter spilled from every corner. But beneath the joy, the air was sharp.

Especially around Rishav.

It happened during a dance practice for the baaraat. Aneri stood with her cousins, laughing as they tried to nail the steps. Viraaj watched from the side lines, his eyes warm, and a smile twitching at his lips when she caught his glance. She didn't smile back, not obviously but the sparkle in her eyes answered him.

Rishav noticed.

He stormed over mid-rehearsal; jaw clenched.

"Aneri," he snapped. "What are you doing here? You should be with my family and me, not wasting time with them."

The cousins went still. Aneri's laughter froze.

"I'm rehearsing with my brother's family," she said quietly. "It's his wedding."

"This wedding isn't about you," Rishav hissed. "Stop making yourself the centre of attention."

The words cracked through the courtyard like lightning.

For a beat, no one spoke. Aneri's cheeks flushed, but her eyes stayed steady. She didn't argue further, didn't stoop to his level. She simply lifted her chin, turned away, and continued dancing.

That quiet defiance was louder than any shouting match.

Viraaj clenched his fists at his side; wanting to intervene but when Aneri glanced at him, just once, her eyes said everything. *Don't. Let me do this my way.*

He nodded almost imperceptibly. Their silence, their glance, said what words could not: he trusted her fire, and she trusted his restraint.

Rishav seethed, realizing he'd lost control not just of her, but of the room. Whispers rustled. Relatives shifted uncomfortably.

He stalked away, his mask cracking further.

And though Aneri returned to her cousins, she could feel Viraaj's gaze steadying her, like an anchor. She didn't look back. She didn't need to.

The house was bursting with noise again, but this time, it wasn't dhols or decorators. It was cousins.

I had been cornered. Literally.

"Viraaj bhaiya," one announced, hands on her hips, "we've decided something."

"That's never good," I muttered.

"You and Aneri di are too serious," another declared. "Always sneaking off, whispering, and staring at each other like some Bollywood slow-motion scene."

I choked. "Excuse me?"

"Yes," the smallest cousin piped up, grinning. "So today we're officially your matchmakers!"

Before I could protest, they shoved Aneri into the circle too, guitar still slung across her shoulder. Her eyes widened, then, narrowed.

"Don't," she warned.

"Oh, we will," the oldest cousin said gleefully. "We've planned a game."

The game was ridiculous: charades. But every clue they handed us was absurdly romantic.

"Propose!"
"Sing a love song!"
"Hold hands!"

I stumbled through, blushing furiously, while Aneri retaliated with deadpan sarcasm.

At one point, when the clue was *'staring deeply into each other's eyes'*, we just stood there, refusing.

But then, as the cousins chanted louder, I risked a glance. Aneri met it. And suddenly, the laughter around us faded.

For three heartbeats, it was just her eyes in mine. Quiet. Steady. Saying everything.

We both broke it off at the same time, cheeks hot, as the cousins squealed in triumph.

Eventually, the aunties scolded them back to haldi clean-up duty, and the circle dissolved.

But as I walked away, I caught Aneri's glance again. Just the tiniest smile tugging her lips.

It said: *they're ridiculous... but maybe not wrong.*

And my heart hammered, wordless but full.

Laishaon Dhar Introspects

That evening, as the courtyard settled into a rare calm, Laishon Dhar sought out Viraaj.

“Walk with me,” he said simply.

Viraaj straightened immediately. “Yes Uncle.”

They walked along the edge of the resort garden, lanterns glowing in the mist. Laishon’s silence was heavy at first. Finally, he spoke.

“You’re a journalist,” Laishon said. “And a comedian.” His tone made the second word sound frivolous.

“Yes, Sir,” Viraaj said evenly. “Both.”

“And what good do you think jokes do? When the country drowns in corruption? When politics is nothing but power games?”

Viraaj paused, choosing his words carefully. “Sir, jokes don’t fix corruption. But they make people look at it. Laugh at it. And when people laugh, they aren't afraid. Fear is what keeps the corrupt safe."

Laishon's brows lifted slightly. "So, you think humour is rebellion?"

Viraaj smiled faintly. "Sometimes rebellion. Sometimes healing. Sometimes both."

They spoke of politics, of youth, of the paralysis of privilege. Laishon pressed hard, testing, probing.

"Do you really believe the youth can change the system?" he asked.

"Yes," Viraaj said firmly. "If they write. If they speak. If they refuse to be silent. Change begins with a word."

Laishon's lips pressed into a line — sceptical, yet not dismissive.

From the shadows, Aneri watched, her heart swelling at Viraaj's calm. He wasn't rattled, wasn't performing. He was simply steady, honest.

Finally, Laishon stopped, studying him. "You speak too much like an idealist," he said.

Viraaj met his gaze. "Better that than a cynic, Sir."

For a beat, silence hung. Then, a flicker. Not quite a smile, but not disapproval either. A glimmer of respect, buried deep.

Laishon turned away. "We'll see, Viraaj. We'll see."

Viraaj exhaled shoulders heavy but heart lighter. He glanced once toward where Aneri stood half-hidden. She met his gaze, her eyes shining with pride.

No words. No smiles. Just a look that said everything.

Rishav's Countermove

Rishav had been watching. Always watching.

The laughter of cousins, the conspiratorial glances, the way Aneri smiled more in Viraaj's presence than in his. It stung. And worse, it made him look weak.

So, he decided to act.

The next morning, as decorators strung marigolds for the wedding mandap, Rishav arrived in a gleaming SUV. His parents followed, bodyguards trailing like shadows.

From the back seat of the car, he unveiled his gift: a massive gold necklace set, dazzling in the sun.

"For my future bride," he announced, slipping it towards Aneri in front of half the family.

Gasps rippled through the courtyard. Aunties oohed. Uncles murmured.

But Aneri froze.

"I... can't accept this," she said firmly. "It's my cousin's wedding. This is her moment, not mine."

Her refusal sliced the air.

Rishav's smile faltered. "You're refusing me? In front of everyone?"

Laishon Dhar stepped in; his voice calm but cold. "This isn't the time, Rishav. Put it away."

For a moment, Rishav's jaw clenched so hard it seemed he might explode. But then he plastered on his politician's smile again and withdrew; the gesture landing flat.

Relatives exchanged looks. Whispers grew.

And in the crowd, Viraaj stood quietly, his eyes steady on Aneri. She met his gaze for just a moment — a silent thank you, a wordless reassurance.

Rishav retreated, but the damage was done. His attempt at grandeur had made him look small.

And though no one said it aloud, the balance was shifting. Slowly. Quietly towards truth.

Laishon Observes Again

The house pulsed with the chaos of mandap preparations — marigolds strung over bamboo frames, priests muttering under their breath about auspicious timings, children darting through corridors carrying trays they had no business touching.

Laishon Dhar stood at the edge of it all, his expression unreadable.

But his mind was restless.

He thought of Rishav's gift — the gold necklace shoved forward like a trophy. He thought of his snapping temper during rehearsals. He thought of Aneri's steady refusal.

And then, inevitably, he thought of Viraaj.

The boy hadn't made grand gestures. He hadn't flaunted wealth or influence. He hadn't raised his voice even when provoked.

Yet Laishon couldn't deny it: in Viraaj's quiet humour, in his thoughtful answers, in the way Aneri seemed lighter in his presence — there was something steady. Something Rishav lacked.

Still, he resisted. Politics mattered. Connections mattered. Rishav's family had both.

But dignity mattered too. And though Laishon had not admitted it aloud, he had begun to fear what kind of life his daughter would lead under a man like Rishav.

Maybe... maybe I've been looking at the wrong measures, he thought, unsettled.

As he turned back toward the mandap-in-progress, he caught sight of Aneri across the courtyard, laughing at something Viraaj had said, her hand brushing her guitar strap.

It was a fleeting image, but it lodged deep in him: his daughter alive, unburdened, herself.

And though he still held his doubts, the seed had grown.

Tension at Dinner and a Realization

That evening, the extended families gathered in the hall for dinner. The air buzzed with exhaustion and anticipation — priests confirming the baaraat's timing, aunties fussing over outfits, cousins sneaking extra gulaab jaamoons.

Rishav sat at the main table with his parents, his jaw tight. The day had not gone his way, and it showed.

It began with something small.

A waiter spilled a little daal while serving. Barely a drop.

Rishav slammed his palm on the table. "Can't you idiots do anything right?" he barked.

The hall froze. The waiter's hands shook.

Viraaj, seated a few chairs away, leaned forward calmly. "It's just daal," he said softly. "No harm done."

The waiter gave him a grateful glance before hurrying away.

But Rishav's fury turned toward Viraaj. "Of course, you'd say that. Always playing the saint. Always trying to look better than me."

Viraaj didn't flinch. He simply lifted his glass of water — not milk this time — and said evenly, "I don't need to look better than anyone. I just don't believe in shouting at people doing their jobs."

A ripple of murmurs ran through the hall.

Aneri's chest tightened.

But it was Laishon Dhar whose gaze lingered the longest. He said nothing, but he saw everything: Rishav's cruelty, Viraaj's steadiness.

And, though he held his silence, his decision edged closer to changing.

Dinner resumed awkwardly, laughter forced, conversations brittle. But beneath it all, the contrast had been drawn in ink.

And once seen, it could not be unseen.

The house was quiet, finally. The drums silenced, the chatter gone, the mandap standing half-finished under the stars.

But Laishon Dhar did not sleep.

He sat by the window of his study, glasses perched low on his nose, a single lamp burning beside him. The papers in front of him — government briefs, half-read — remained untouched. His thoughts wandered elsewhere.

He replayed the dinner in his mind.

The waiter's trembling hands.
Rishav's voice, sharp and cruel.
Viraaj's calm, steady words.

I don't need to look better than anyone. I just don't believe in shouting at people doing their jobs.

The line lingered, refusing to leave.

Laishon rubbed his temple. Rishav's family carried weight. Political influence. Security. The kind of alliance any father would be proud of.

And yet...

What kind of home would Aneri have, tied to a man who shouted at waiters? Who saw service as servitude, not dignity?

In his silence, Laishon admitted the truth he'd been resisting: respect mattered more than power.

And though he had not spoken it aloud, he knew what his heart was telling him.

When he thought of Aneri laughing with her guitar, her eyes brighter around Viraaj, a ghost of a smile tugged his lips.

Perhaps, he thought reluctantly, the boy wasn't so foolish after all.

Still, he shut his lamp, burying the thought under layers of duty.

But deep down, he knew: the cracks in his resolve were widening.

Rishav's Boiling Point

Across town, in the guest quarters where Rishav and his family stayed, the mood was anything but quiet.

Rishav paced the floor like a caged animal, his parents seated stiffly on the sofa. His bodyguards loomed near the door, silent shadows.

"That boy," Rishav spat. "That milk-drinking buffoon. Always hovering. Always pretending to be better. And did you see her? Did you see how she looked at him instead of me?"

His mother sighed. "You're letting this get to you. Focus on the bigger picture."

"The bigger picture?" he barked. "I'm being humiliated in front of her entire family! If they see me as weak, if she dares to defy me—"

His father cut him off sharply. "Control yourself. Politics is about image. Don't lose it."

But Rishav only clenched his fists tighter.

He turned to his goons. "Tomorrow, I don't care how. I want him gone. Do whatever it takes."

The men nodded silently, their eyes glinting.

Rishav sank into a chair, his breath ragged. "She's mine. Do you hear me? Mine. And no journalist comedian from Chennai will steal her away."

His voice echoed in the small room, heavy with rage.

And in the shadows, the storm began to take shape.

The mandap rose higher by the hour — bamboo poles wrapped in cloth, marigolds strung like rivers of gold, priests muttering timing debates.

I had been roped into helping string fairy lights, clumsy but determined, perched on a ladder. Aneri hovered nearby with cousins, laughing at my "decorator's stance."

That's when they came.

Two of Rishav's men sidled up, pretending to carry supplies. But their eyes were sharp, their shoulders heavy with intent.

"You," one muttered up at me. "Journalist boy. A word."

I climbed down slowly. "Yes?"

The other leaned close. "You don't belong here. Stop interfering. Stay out of Miss Aneri's way — or you'll regret it."

Before I could reply, the fairy lights above sparked. I looked up just in time to see a fuse about to blow.

On instinct, I grabbed a loose wire, twisted it back into place, and the entire mandap lit up in a spectacular burst — golden lights shimmering across the courtyard.

Gasps. Cheers. Even the priest clapped.

The goons scowled; their intimidation lost in the applause. One muttered, "Lucky fool," before retreating.

Aneri's eyes found mine, shining. She didn't say anything. She didn't need to. The pride in her glance was louder than words.

Later, while the courtyard swarmed with relatives fixing flowers and priests squabbling over timing, Laishon Dhar stood at the veranda, arms folded.

He had seen everything.

Rishav hovered near the elders, his smile stretched, his voice dripping politeness. But it was stiff, calculated, rehearsed. He looked like a man attending a press conference, not a wedding.

Meanwhile, across the courtyard, Viraaj was being ambushed by cousins with marigold petals. He flailed; ducked, cracked jokes — and Aneri, laughing so freely beside him didn't even notice she was glowing.

The contrast was stark. One forced. One effortless.

Laishon's jaw tightened.

He didn't want to admit it but somewhere deep, the truth gnawed: his daughter was herself with Viraaj. Alive and unmasked.

And wasn't that worth more than any alliance?

He said nothing, but the thought lodged heavier than ever.

Aneri's Quiet Reflection

That night, the hills were hushed. The mandap stood nearly finished, glowing faintly under lanterns.

In her room, Aneri strummed her guitar softly, her thoughts spiralling.

Viraaj doesn't even try. He doesn't perform. He just... is.

She remembered him on the ladder, fairy lights sparking, calmly fixing the wire as if chaos was second nature. She remembered the cousins' mischief, how he stumbled yet always laughed at himself first.

She remembered his silences — the way he never demanded words, but always answered hers with a glance, a nod, a steady presence.

I never said it. He never said it. But it's already there. Isn't it?

Her hand stilled on the strings.

For the first time, Aneri admitted it to herself. Quietly. Fiercely.

She loved him.

And she didn't need to say it aloud to know he already did too.

The resort had transformed overnight. The mandap glittered with marigolds, brass lamps polished to a glow. Tailors rushed through corridors, priests barked timings, and cousins danced through the hallways singing snippets of Bollywood songs.

The baaraat was almost ready.

In the chaos, Viraaj and Aneri found their moments.

When everyone was distracted, he stole her dupatta to "protect" it from the turmeric stains flying around, holding it up like a flag until she snatched it back with a laugh.

Later, when she carried her guitar across the courtyard, he walked beside her in silence, their shoulders almost brushing.

"You know," he said casually, "I think your guitar likes me more than you do."

"Unlikely," she replied dryly but her smile gave her away.

In the kitchen, amid trays of sweets, he found her struggling to balance three plates at once. He slipped one easily from her hands, earning a quiet, "Thanks."

They stood there a second too long, caught in each other's gaze, before a cousin barged in and the spell broke.

It wasn't grand. It wasn't dramatic. But every glance, every brush of laughter, stitched them closer.

From a distance, Laishon Dhar noticed again. He said nothing, but each time his daughter smiled at Viraaj, his silence grew heavier, less certain.

And though Aneri and Viraaj never uttered the word 'love,' it was already written in the spaces between them.

The Ambush and the Baaraat Explosion

The baaraat drums were already warming up in the distance when it happened.

I had gone out toward the back of the resort to fetch an extension cord for the DJ's setup — a mundane task, nothing heroic. But the moment I rounded the corner, I felt it: the silence was wrong.

And then, they stepped out.

Three of Rishav's men.

"Journalist boy," one sneered, "Time to learn your place."

The first swung a fist. I ducked instinctively — years of kabaddi training snapping to life. The man's punch hit a wall instead, and he howled.

The second lunged. I sidestepped, grabbing a broken broomstick nearby. Not as a weapon, just... instinct. The man tripped over a cable and tumbled into the crates of marigolds.

By the time the third came at me, I'd already wired the extension cord — and sparks flew, scaring him so badly he stumbled back into a bucket of haldi water.

When it was over, I stood there panting, broomstick in hand, fairy lights glowing behind me like a halo. The goons groaned in turmeric, marigolds, and sparks.

The DJ peeked out. "What happened?"

"Just... stage practice," I muttered, brushing marigold petals off my shirt.

But when I turned, Aneri was there, her guitar case at her side, eyes wide. She hadn't seen every detail, but enough.

Her lips curved the smallest smile.

"You always find trouble, don't you?" she said softly.

"Or it finds me," I replied.

No more words. But her gaze lingered, filled with something unspoken —worry, and a tenderness that made my chest ache.

The drums thundered. The baraat had begun.

Arvind (the groom, Aneri's cousin) sat nervously astride the decorated horse, cousins dancing wildly in front, dhol players pounding with enough force to shake the hills. The mandap glittered in the distance, a marigold crown waiting for him.

I had been roped into walking with the cousins, holding up a lantern-stick I didn't quite know how to wave. I looked ridiculous — but the cousins cheered me on anyway.

Everything was pure chaos until the wrong kind of chaos arrived.

Through the mist of fireworks and drum smoke, I saw them: Rishav's men again, lurking at the edge of the procession.

Too late, I realized what they were about to do.

One lunged forward, trying to shove me into the dhol wall. Another grabbed my sleeve.

The cousins screamed, the drums faltered, and for a second, the baraat teetered on panic.

But instinct kicked in.

The first goon lunged — I ducked low, sweeping his leg like a kabaddi tackle. He crashed into the gulaab jaamoons cart, the sweets exploding across the street.

The second swung a fist — I dodged, and his hand landed in the cymbals, the clang so loud it made him stumble back holding his ears.

The third grabbed me from behind — but I twisted free, accidentally yanking the extension cord from the DJ setup. Sparks flew, music screeched — and then, miraculously, the backup speakers boomed to life with a thundering Bollywood track.

The cousins roared. "Dance fight!"

And suddenly, instead of panic, the baraat turned into a riot of laughter.

The cousins dragged me into the dance circle, spinning me away from the goons. One tripped on marigold petals, another slipped in the gulaab jaamoons mess, and before long, the three of them had been tossed around the baraat like clowns in a circus.

The dhol players picked up the beat, louder than ever. Fireworks burst above.

By the time the priests caught up, the baaraat looked unstoppable — a tidal wave of sound, colour, and chaos.

From the mandap entrance, Aneri stood watching. Her eyes never left me, even as the whole crowd moved.

I hadn't done it gracefully. I hadn't done it perfectly. But I had kept the baaraat moving.

And when her gaze caught mine across the crowd, it was like the whole noise fell away. Just a look. Just a spark. Just us.

The goons slunk away, humiliated. Rishav, watching from a distance, clenched his jaw so tight I thought it might break.

But the baaraat only grew louder.

And in the middle of it, covered in petals and sweat, I realized something: I wasn't just part of their chaos anymore. I belonged here.

Rishav's Public Snap

The courtyard buzzed with fevered energy. Priests barked instructions, cousins argued about missing flower garlands, and the mandap gleamed under fairy lights.

In the midst of it all, Rishav's patience finally crumbled.

It started when Aneri stepped aside to tune her guitar. She was supposed to play softly during one of the rituals, a small musical offering — her way of honouring her cousin's wedding.

But to Rishav, it was another chance for her to slip out of his orbit.

"Again, with that guitar?" he hissed, too sharply for a man pretending to charm. "Do you ever put it down? You think this is your stage?"

The crowd went still. Too many heard it this time.

Aneri didn't answer. She didn't need to. She straightened, placed her hand gently on the strings, and strummed one quiet note; A defiant, graceful sound that seemed to hang in the mist.

The cousins exchanged looks. The aunties pursed their lips. Rishav flushed, realizing too late how much he had revealed.

Viraaj stood near the mandap steps, silent, his eyes fixed on Aneri. He didn't move, didn't speak. But his gaze was steady, protective — a wall without words.

And Aneri's eyes flicked to his, just once, drawing strength from the silent bridge between them.

Rishav forced a smile, mumbling something about "nerves" to the elders. But the damage was done. Whispers spread, sharper now, harder to dismiss.

And though no declaration was made, everyone saw the truth.

It happened the next day, as the mandap was dressed in its final garlands, the baaraat minutes away.

Rishav cornered Aneri near the side corridor, voice low but venomous.

"You embarrassed me again. Once more and I swear—"

"Swear what?" a voice cut in.

Laishon Dhar stepped forward, his presence calm but unyielding. For a moment, even the drums seemed to pause.

"This is my daughter's wedding home," he said evenly. "Not yours. If you cannot respect her, I shall consider this disrespect to me. Do I make myself clear?"

Rishav stammered, caught between rage and the weight of Laishon's authority. His parents weren't nearby to shield him. His goons weren't nearby to intimidate.

And Aneri, for the first time — looked at her father not with fear, but with gratitude.

Later, as he walked back to the mandap, Laishon's thoughts churned.

He thought of the girl his daughter had become in Chennai — a marketing team leader, sharp and capable, someone who had refused to remain just a professor, and someone who had chosen her own path. He thought of how her music wasn't just a hobby but a voice.

She wasn't a prize. She wasn't a pawn. She was her own person.

And for the first time, Laishon admitted it to himself fully:

She needed someone who saw her that way.

Someone like Viraaj.

Across the courtyard, he caught sight of Viraaj again — half helping with decorations, half joking with cousins, never trying to centre himself yet somehow drawing the centre to him.

Laishon exhaled. The scales inside him had tipped.

Not fully. Not openly but undeniably.

The Wedding Dawns

The sun rose over the Shillong hills like a drumbeat.

The baaraat had arrived. The horse was decked in flowers, the dhols roared, cousins twirled in bright silks. The mandap gleamed, draped in marigolds and golden cloth, glowing against the mist.

The bride and groom — Riya and Arvind — were radiant, the centre of the world.

But beneath the laughter, beneath the music, tension thrummed.

I stood near the edge of the mandap, helping cousins carry trays of flowers. Aneri moved gracefully among her family, her dupatta brushing the air like a flame.

Every glance we exchanged was a whisper, a reassurance.

But across the courtyard, Rishav stood too. His eyes never left us. His smile was stretched too thin. And behind him, his men shifted, waiting.

The priests called for the families to gather. The pheres were minutes away.

The crowd bustled, laughter rose, bells rang.

But beneath it all, the air vibrated with something else. Something about to break.

Tomorrow had arrived.

The mandap was glowing, the fire already lit, priests chanting. The pheras (seven rounds around the sacred fire in the Hindu ritual of marriage) were moments away.

"Viraaj beta, Aneri," one of the aunties called, "the kalash (a ceremonial pot used in Hindu rituals) of holy water — it's still near the storeroom! Quick, bring it here before the rituals begin."

We nodded, slipping away through the side corridor. The main courtyard was too crowded, too loud. Here, the path was quieter, the lanterns dimmer.

That's when I felt it — the wrong kind of silence.

From the shadows, a group of burly looking men stepped out. Rishav's men.

"Well, well," one sneered. "Running errands now, journalist boy? Thought you'd be the hero?"

Before I could reply, another lunged for the kalash in my hands.

I ducked, pivoting instinctively, the man crashing into the wall. Another swung at me — I sidestepped, my kabaddi instincts firing, and he tumbled into a tray of flower garlands.

The third tried to grab Aneri. But before I could reach her, she swung her guitar case with surprising force. It connected with a hollow *thunk*, sending him staggering back.

"You picked the wrong corridor," she muttered under her breath.

I swung the kalash like a shield, deflecting another grab. Water sloshed dangerously. Sparks flew as one of them tripped over a hanging string of lights, shocking himself and yelping.

In the madness, I spotted a loose extension wire dangling near the floor. Without thinking, I twisted it back into its socket, and the entire corridor lit up, blinding the goons.

They stumbled, dazed, muttering curses as they fled into the dark.

I exhaled hard, glancing at Aneri. She was breathless but steady, the kalash still safe between us.

We didn't speak. We didn't need to.

Together, we carried it back to the mandap.

Just as the priest raised his hand, we placed the kalash at his feet. He nodded, satisfied, as if nothing had happened.

The crowd hushed. Riya and Arvind circled the fire, step by step, vow by vow. The chanting rose, bells rang, and for those moments, the world was only light and flame.

No shadows intruded. No chaos broke through.

Love stood untouched.

Later, as the bride's side wept and laughed in equal measure, Riya hugged everyone — uncles, aunties, cousins — tears streaming but a smile never leaving her lips.

The bidaai (a Hindu ritual where the bride bids goodbye to her parental home before leaving for her husband's home) wasn't a departure across miles, but across courtyards. With her husband, she walked toward the groom's family cottages for the post-wedding puja, her dupatta trailing like a shimmering river of red.

We clapped, cheered, cried. And though the distance was small, the meaning was vast.

Through it all, Aneri stood beside me, her face glowing in the firelight. I caught her glance once, and she held it, steady and sure.

We had carried more than a kalash tonight.

We had carried something unspoken — and unbreakable.

The Showdown

The bidaai had ended, the bride gone toward her new courtyard, tears trailing behind her laughter. The family slowly dispersed the air heavy with relief and exhaustion.

But not everyone was done.

Rishav.

He stood near the gate, his face pale with rage, his parents behind him whispering caution. The moment the elders thinned, he stepped forward, his voice cutting across the night.

So, this is it?" he barked. "The wedding is done, and I'm treated like a guest in the shadows? After everything my family has offered you?"

The courtyard froze.

Laishon Dhar's jaw tightened, but he said nothing yet.

"You all laugh, you all cheer," Rishav spat, "while *he—*" his finger jabbed at me, "that clown ruins everything. What does he have? What does he offer? A milk glass and a bundle of bad jokes?"

Murmurs rippled. Eyes darted between us.

Aneri stepped forward before I could. Her voice was calm, sharp as steel.

"What he offers," she said, "is respect. Something you've never understood."

The courtyard gasped. Rishav's face burned crimson.

"You dare—" he lunged, not at me, but at Laishon, fury spilling beyond control.

But before he could touch him, I moved, stepping between them, hand outstretched. "Enough."

The silence was electric. Rishav panted his mask in pieces. And in the crowd, the last of his influence shattered.

His parents tugged at him, urging him back, muttering about dignity. But the whispers had already spread, the truth already written: this was no suitor. This was a tyrant unmasked.

And as his goons hovered uncertainly, waiting for orders, the weight of eyes on them forced retreat.

Rishav was livid with rage.

"You think this is over?" he snarled, shoving me back. "You humiliated me. You made me a fool. Now I'll show you what happens when someone crosses me."

His fist connected with my jaw, hard. Pain flared, metallic and hot.

I staggered. Another hit landed on my ribs. I doubled but didn't fall.

The crowd gasped, rushing out of cottages. Aneri screamed, "Viraaj!"

I straightened, spit blood, and forced a grin. "That all you got, Rishav? I thought politicians' sons had better training."

We collided. Fists, sweat and fury. My kabaddi instincts saved me more than once, but I wasn't untouched. My cheek throbbed, my knuckles burned, my body screamed.

Still — I stood.

Suddenly, Laishon Dhar pushed between us, his arm raised.

"Enough! This is not a battlefield; this is my family's place of celebration!"

But Rishav, breathless with rage, jabbed his finger into Laishon's chest. "We had a deal. You'll regret breaking it, old man!"

He raised his hand as if to strike.

Gasps echoed. Aneri cried out.

I shoved Rishav back, my voice carrying across the courtyard.

"You call yourself powerful, Rishav? Power isn't fists. Power isn't screaming. It's respect. It's dignity. And you've never had either. You say I come from nothing? Maybe I do. But at least I know who I am. And that's something you'll never learn."

The crowd erupted, murmuring, nodding.

Rishav sneered. "You can't do anything to me."

I chuckled, blood on my lip. "Can't I?"

A siren blared suddenly. A jeep roared through the gates. Out stepped ATS Chief Sangram "Simba" Bhaalerao, sunglasses gleaming under the floodlights.

"Mahaaraaj ki jai ho!" he shouted, grinning wide.

The crowd gasped. He strode up, shook my hand firmly, and then, turned to his constables.

"Arrest them all — Section 151. Public havoc during a wedding. Now they can take their pheraas in jail."

The crowd laughed nervously as Rishav and his goons were dragged away, kicking and shouting. His parents begged, but Laishon's voice cut sharp:

"Go. There is no place for you here."

Their SUV rolled behind the jeeps; the storm finally broken.

But Simba stayed. He clapped my shoulder.

"You did well, Viraaj. You stood steady. You called me, I came — but even without me, you showed them who you are."

He turned to Aneri, bowing slightly, then, bent to touch her feet. "Yeh toh humaari bhaabhi hui. Paaye lagoo, bhaabhi" (You are my sis in law. Respects to you).

The crowd chuckled, clapping. Aneri blushed, stammering, "Hello, Inspector ji..."

Simba grinned. "Chief now. ATS Chief. But for you, always Simba."

He turned back to the families. "This man comes from a line of courage — his late grandfather, DSP Deenadayal, was a lion of Tamil Nadu Police. My grandfather knew him. Families like theirs taught us what service means. And yet," he squeezed my shoulder, "look at him. Simple, grounded, middle class. That's real royalty. Not power, not money. Simplicity. Truth."

He turned back to me. "Promise me, Viraaj bhai — you'll keep writing. You'll keep laughing. You'll keep fighting the right way."

I nodded voice hoarse. "Always."

He winked. "And when Rohit Shetty makes your biopic, tell him Simba said pranaam (regards)."

With that, his jeep roared into the night.

The storm was over.

The Author Reveal, Public

The next morning, breakfast buzzed with tension and relief. The storm had passed, but ripples still ran through the family.

Then, Laishon Dhar rose, voice solemn.

"As parents, we often forget. We think giving our children wealth is enough. But wealth doesn't raise them. Values do. And yesterday, I saw the difference. I saw what happens when children are given power without respect. And I saw what happens when a child is raised with truth."

He paused, then, quoted:

> "Parents must teach their children to stand in storms, not hide behind walls. Generational wealth crumbles. Generational courage builds nations."

I froze. Those words sounded familiar.

"Sir... you wrote those lines?"

He smiled. "From my favourite author -Shaily Raghuvanshi. Her book, "Arise, Awake & Do Not Scroll", is one of my favourites. It talks about the youth of today, how change is required in the country and in the world. How Technology was meant to help mankind and not cripple it, and a brilliant commentary on the simple life everyone should learn to lead."

The table murmured. Aneri blinked.

I swallowed. "She's, my mother."

The table went silent.

I showed him a photo on my phone — Mumma and I in Chennai, smiling.

Laishon's face softened, his hand trembling slightly. "All these years, I've quoted her, admired her. And now... her son stands here. And I see it. The same truth. The same courage."

His eyes met mine. Publicly. Openly.

"You are not what I feared. You are what I hoped for."

Tears burned my eyes. Aneri's mother clasped my hand. Her uncle and aunt nodded with warm smiles.

And in that moment, acceptance bloomed — not grudging, not reluctant. But real acknowledgment.

Laishon leaned forward. "Tell me, Viraaj... do you write too?"

I smiled faintly. "Yes, Uncle. I'm working on something. A story of rivers and hills, of chaos and love. One day, I'll bring it out."

The crowd clapped softly. Aneri's eyes shone.

And I knew — I belonged.

The Shillong Farewell

The resort slowly emptied, like a dream dissolving at dawn.

Suitcases rolled, cars honked softly, relatives hugged and waved. The hills of Shillong seemed quieter already, as if they too had exhaled after the storm.

I stood at the veranda with Aneri, both of us watching as her parents came forward.

Laishon Dhar and his wife blessed us; their palms warm on our heads. "Be good," her mother whispered. Laishon only nodded his eyes serious but no longer conflicted.

Then they left, their car fading into the morning mist.

For a moment, Aneri and I stood in silence, shoulders brushing, a quiet joy humming between us. We were leaving together, to the same destination — Chennai.

As the porter carried our bags, Aneri's phone buzzed. She frowned, stepped aside, whispered into it.

When she returned, her smile was faint but strained. "Viraaj... I need to go somewhere first. Urgently. Baba asked me. Our train's later, we'll manage. We can go together, or you can come along and wait."

I hesitated, but her voice was firm. "It won't take long. Please."

I agreed.

We returned to her childhood home briefly, a house filled with old photos and guitar cases stacked in corners. Aneri went upstairs to change.

My phone rang — my editor in Chennai.

"Viraaj, it's perfect you are in Shillong. PDP (People's Democratic Party) is making history today — youngest political member in North East ever. Big press meets. You must cover it."

"Now?"

"Yes. Go. Write. Ask. Shake them."

I sighed, smiling faintly. The timing was absurd. But wasn't that my life?

I ducked into a spare bathroom, changing into khadi kurta and jeans.

When I came out, I saw Aneri; she was looking radiant, full-sleeved blouse saari carrying both grace and command.

"You look..." I stammered.

"So do you," she cut in, eyes sparkling.

We smiled. Then we left, sliding into her father's car. The driver started the engine.

"The press meet is in that office building near the market," I said, checking my message.

She blinked, surprised. "That's where I have to go too. Lots of press things happen there."

She leaned against me, her hands wrapping around my arm, her head resting on my shoulder. I caressed her hand, warmth filling my chest.

Neither of us said more. Neither of us knew.

We reached the building. At the entrance, signs split left and right.

She paused. "I go left."

I nodded. "I go right."

We hugged quickly. She pulled out her phone. "Wait — number?"

We exchanged digits. To test it, she dialled. My phone blared *Badtameez Dil*.

She chuckled, shaking her head. "Of course."

"Don't judge," I grinned.

We parted ways.

My press ID hung around my neck. Other journalists gawked.

"A Tamil Nadu journalist? Here? Already?"

"I was here for a wedding," I said with a shrug.

I sat near the back; notebook ready.

On stage, four chairs gleamed. An old man with a heavy moustache approached the podium.

"Today," he boomed, "is a proud day for the People's Democratic Party. For years, Mr. Dhar has supported us with wisdom and strength. And today, with a vacancy left by someone's resignation, we appoint the youngest political member in the history of the North East."

Cameras clicked wildly.

"Please welcome... Aneri Khongwir."

The room erupted.

I froze.

She stepped onto the stage, smiling, poised, and radiant. Flashbulbs lit her like fire.

I stood too slowly, still staring. She noticed me instantly. Our eyes locked across the hall, stunned.

Neither of us sat.

Neither of us looked away.

The old man cleared his throat. "Do you have a question, young man?"

I blinked, realizing all eyes were on me.

And then, softly, from the security guard's phone at the back of the hall, a song floated through the chaos — "Ajeeb Daastan Hai Yeh" by Lata Mangeshkar.

It's a strange story,
where it begins, where it ends,
we cannot know...

The words were knives and balm all at once.

A strange story. Yes. Ours.

One a politician. The other a journalist.

And, as we stared at each other, one question thundering in both our minds:

How is this going to work? What next?

The cameras clicked, the song played, the world tilted.

And I knew this was only the beginning.

Acknowledgements

This book is the fruit of countless blessings, lessons, and journeys.

First, I bow in gratitude to the places that have shaped me—Salem, Madras, Palakkad, Madurai and India. Each of these lands has been a teacher in its own way, gifting me with wisdom, memories, and inspiration that have found their way into these pages.

To Nature, my eternal guide, and to the many animals who adopted me along the way—Choti Cat, the kittens, the stray dogs, Jobi, the goldfishes, the parrots, the woodpeckers, the squirrels, and so many others—thank you for your companionship, your presence, and the silent lessons you shared.

To my teachers—from school to college, I am forever indebted. To my well-wishers, who believed in me even when I faltered, thank you.

To my father, Mr. D. Om Prakash, who has been the wellspring of my curiosity and imagination, and to my mother, Ms. Shail Raghuvanshi, who inspired me to write—I owe everything. Together, you have been my greatest guides, my strongest supporters, and my truest best friends. I carry your love in every dream I chase.

To **Mr. Hemant Bansal of FanatiXx Publication**, my publisher, thank you for walking beside me on this journey.

To all the friends of my father and the friends of my mother—your kindness and encouragement have meant more than words can say.

To the hardships and lessons of life, I extend gratitude too, for without them I would not be standing here today.

To every house I called home, and to every relative—past and present—who wished the best for me, thank you for being part of my journey.

To my maternal grandfather, Shri. S. P. Singh (Naanu), whose wisdom, support, and strength even at 91 continues to guide me—I owe my understanding of savings, money, and finance to you.

To my late maternal grandmother, Smt. Kamala Pandey (Naani), thank you for the nurturing love that taught me to cherish human connections.

To my late paternal grandfather, Shri. L. Deenadayal (Thaata), whose life of disciplined police service, mastery of Kriya Yoga, and knowledge of astrology inspires me endlessly—I carry forward your legacy with joy, curiosity, and kindness.

To my late paternal grandmother, Smt. Sundari Dayal (Paati), whose love and affection shaped my understanding of compassion, I remain forever grateful.

Above all, to the Divine Energy—the Universe—my dearest friend and constant companion. Thank you for the gift of human birth, for this wondrous life, and for always having my back.

Vinod Naraen – Author

Vinod Naraen has worked as a journalist, a copywriter and a stand-up comedian before discovering his true passion for writing.

He has interests in music, cinema, mythology and research.

He lives in Chennai with his family.

This is his first book which is a part of a trilogy series.

Part 1 of Trilogy

The END

www.ingramcontent.com/pod-product-compliance
Lightning Source LLC
Chambersburg PA
CBHW050525240926
51846CB00003B/692
* 9 7 8 9 3 7 4 0 6 9 5 5 4 *